WARPED CONDUIT

MISSION SIX

JOHN P. LOGSDON

CHRISTOPHER P. YOUNG

CRIMSON MYTH PRESS

Copyright © 2015 by John P. Logsdon & Christopher P. Young

Published by: Crimson Myth Press (www.CrimsonMyth.com)

Cover art: Jake T. Logsdon (www.JakeLogsdon.com)

Acknowledgments

As always, thanks to friends and family for putting up with the ever-distant author's mind. It's really better this way, though, because you honestly don't want to know what we're thinking in real-time.

An enormous *Thank You!* goes to our awesome launch team (listed in order of joining):

David Ridgway, Richard Doubleday, Jamie Duke, Tony Dawson, Christopher Ridgway, Mike Ridgway, Michelle Dupree, Sean Ellis, Nick Moon, Julia Taylor, Neil Gurling, Leigh Evans, David Buckle, Joe Simon, Andy Riley, John Ladbury, Alex Ochs McKenzie, Athena Stringfellow, Helen Wrenn, Geoffrey Ackers, Tony Dodds, James Hannah, Terry Foster, J. Ed Baker, James Goddard, Kim Phelan, Paul McCarthy, Steve Hayes, David Williamson, Cher Eaves, Barrie Mee, Joel Jackson, Darrell Northcott, Linda Carter, Stephen A. Smith, Erin Mattox, Jennie Nichols, Jodie Stackowiak, John Debnam, Stuart Horsfall, Keith Hall, Neil Lowrie, Ronnie Beaton, Stuart Faulkner, Madeleine Fenner, Adam Pederick, Arto Suokas, Sirene Cleife, Terri Innes, Nicola Garrately-White, Eric Hirsch, Phyllis McGrath, Virna Thibault, Nic Jensen, and Paul Ladmore.

UNDER ATTACK

Captain Don Harr slammed into his command chair as a barrage of missiles struck the side of his ship. The *SSMC Reluctant* hadn't been built to handle this type of abuse. She was a ship meant to be attached to rails in space. Yes, it was idiocy, but that's how things were done on Harr's home planet of Segnal.

"Any idea where the hell these guys came from?" he asked to nobody in particular.

"No, sir," answered his second-in-command, Kip Sandoo, who stood tall with his hands clasped behind his back, his strong jaw pointed toward the main screen.

Another jolt nearly took Harr completely out of the chair. He struggled to right himself while the rest of his crew barely budged, holding themselves in place as if nothing had happened. To be fair, they were all androids. They had the strength to brace themselves in the roughest situations. Harr didn't have that luxury seeing that he was the only human aboard.

"You should put your seatbelt on, sir," Commander Sandoo suggested.

"If I can get situated for more than two seconds, Commander, I'll do just that." Fortunately, he got just enough of a reprieve to click his belt in place before the next explosion, and then he slammed his fist on the button that activated the intercom on his chair. "Geezer," he called down to engineering, "can you get us the hell out of here before these ships destroy us?"

"No can do, chief," Geezer replied in the only attitude-laced monotone voice that Harr had ever heard. Considered antiquated even by robotic standards on Segnal, Geezer came from the G.3.3.Z.3.R. line, meaning that he had attitude and good old-fashioned engineering skills. He was the epitome of the old style robot, including the spindly arms, blocky torso, and little antennas sticking off his square head. He was the only other non-android on the *Reluctant*. "I'm fighting enough just to keep our circuits humming. Shields are dropping pretty damn fast. At this rate, they'll be dead pretty soon."

"So will we."

"Thir," Lieutenant Hank Moon said in his lisped way, "it looks like they're attacking in a standard delta pattern." The lisp wasn't consistent, but then again neither was Hank Moon. He inhabited one of the most perfect female specimens Harr had ever laid eyes on. Dark skin, firm body, long legs, beautiful smile, and a great mind. He had started out as a she, or, more accurately, a *they* that consisted of three distinct personalities, but on that fateful day when Geezer was finally able to meld all three of those personalities into one, Hank Moon rose to the top and became the final representative.

"Standard delta, you say?"

"Yes, thir."

"I see," Harr said, though he didn't. "Is that useful information?"

"It is, thir," Hank said, turning back to look at him. "We could counter them with an Alpha-Theta-3-1-Switch."

Harr blinked at Moon as his mind struggled to recall exactly what an Alpha-Theta-3-1-Switch looked like.

"Okay," he said, hopefully, "do that."

"I don't know how, thir."

"Then what was the purpose of bringing it up, Lieutenant?"

"I thought maybe you knew the maneuver."

"And I probably should," Harr replied before the ship took another hit. This one was just a graze, but it kept them in the game. "My cadet training was some years ago, Lieutenant. Certainly there's something on the computer that details this, right?"

Lieutenant Brekka Ridly spun in her chair, looking a bit more soldierly than Lieutenant Moon. Where Moon was quite curvy, wore makeup, and did his hair in various fashions, depending on the day, Ridly was muscular, kept her skin free of cosmetics, and had only one hairstyle: cropped.

"Sir," she said, "the Alpha-Theta-3-1-Switch is a just a reverse thrust move."

"Could you expand on that a little bit?"

"Basically, we reverse the polarity of the magnetism on propulsion. The ship will screech to a halt on the rails and then send us screaming backward while the enemy ships zip on by. Then we can light them up from behind."

"I see," said Harr while he pursed his lips and tapped his first finger on the bridge of his nose. "Makes perfect sense, except for the bit where we're no longer on rails, Lieutenant."

"Oh yeah," Ridly replied. "Forgot about that."

A blast caused Harr's head to flip backward, giving him a bit of whiplash. It was the worst strike yet, strong enough to set a few of the main panels aflame.

Ensigns Grover Curr and Miles Middleton grabbed

extinguishers and started putting out one of the fires that flared up on the secondary access panel that sat by the hatch.

"I'm already working on this one, you ass," Middleton, the larger of the two, said to Curr.

"I was here first, jerk," Curr replied as he tried to muscle Middleton out of the way. "Go work on the other one!"

The two ensigns had been relatively quiet during the first few missions that the *Reluctant* had run, but they'd grown more and more agitated with each other as the days rolled on. There were times where Harr thought there would be an all-out brawl between the two.

By now, Ensign Brand Jezden had joined in to help put out the flames. Jezden was the one that Harr had the most issues with. He was insubordinate, had a bad attitude, rubbed most of the men the wrong way, and rubbed most of the women the right way—assuming they allowed him to, which they most often did. To say he was good-looking was an understatement, but it was what he packed in his groin region that made every man within a light year feel inadequate in comparison. Put it this way: the android had won the coveted *Steel Bone Award* for his participation at the Loose Box Porno Convention on the planet Klood.

"Are we at least firing back?" Harr asked. "Please tell me somebody has taken the initiative on that."

They glanced around at each other.

"Seriously? Come on, gang. You're supposed to be soldiers!"

THE OVERSEERS

*T*he room was mostly dark as the Overseers, in general, did not like to be seen. Some were less conspicuous than others, but many were hidden under dark archways that were purposefully set in shadows.

Frexle stood before them, ready to give his monthly report on the status of the nation. The nation being the group of hand-selected people from various races in the universe. Frexle was one of the few who had access to records on every member, and so he knew the level of representation for each major population sector. There were only 143,927 citizens in all, including spouses, offspring, and oftentimes members of their respective extended families. The panel consisted of 14 members.

"My esteemed colleagues," he said strongly, trying to hide his apprehension, "the *HadItWithTheKillings* political party is rising in popularity."

"Damn liberals," Veli, the Lord Overseer, said with a grumble. "Who cares what they think?"

Murmurs from the rest of the panel indicated their agreement.

"Normally I would agree, my lord," Frexle said carefully, "but their support is steadily increasing among the populace. Last year they were at five percent, last month it was twenty-five percent, and an hour ago they had climbed to thirty-three percent."

"That's still not enough to challenge the current party, Frexle," said Senator Calloom.

"Very true, Senator. However, it's becoming increasingly clear that their rate of support is significant. Jumping eight points in a single month is dangerous. The recent rate of acceptance postulates that they will hit fifty percent support in a matter of months."

Senator Pookand stood up and placed his frail hands on the podium that stood in front of his chair. "We'll just put out some new pictures of ourselves playing a round of golf on Landumbi like we did before the last elections."

"Excellent idea," said Calloom. "That gave us a solid three percent bump last time."

"We could also release a set of new posters," Senator Kleeve suggested. "The people love posters, especially if we put our faces on them."

Frexle thought that it was a decent idea as well, except that the only senators who had ever been insane enough to show their faces to the general populace were Pookand, Calloom, and Kleeve.

"Yes," Pookand agreed. "Or we could make the posters poke fun at the *HadItWithTheKillings* group."

"Capital idea, Senator Pookand," Kleeve said as she jotted a note on her datapad. "I hadn't thought of using attack tactics."

"Posters and photo ops are clever and cute," Veli chimed in, "but I feel that an assassination is in order." The senators seemed to find this idea the most appealing of them all. "Frexle, what do we know of their leadership?"

"Not much, Lord Overseer," Frexle answered apologetically. "It's an underground movement. Their message moves through hidden channels via untraceable routes. They are very clever, I'm afraid."

"Do they even *have* a leader?"

"If they do, my lord, he or she is well disguised." There was a moment of silence. Then, Frexle said, "Sometimes all that's needed is an idea to change the course of history."

"I hate ideas," Veli grumbled, "except those that are my own, of course. Hard to kill an idea, though I have killed tougher things."

"Ideas are easily destroyed by pointing out their ridiculousness," Pookand said.

"True," Veli said. "What's the idea again, Frexle?"

"That we shouldn't simply wipe out a civilization because they are progressing in a direction that may threaten our superiority, Lord Overseer."

"Wait, that's it?" asked Kleeve, leaning forward just enough so that Frexle could make out her pallid green skin.

"Yes, ma'am."

"What do they expect us to do?"

"Uh...not wipe out complete civilizations anymore?"

"Don't get snarky with me, young man," Kleeve admonished. "My point is that the council is tasked with making sure that no group, race, world, or what have you, ever comes close to dethroning our great empire, right?" Frexle nodded. "So when we see some snotty little upstart getting close to a discovery that will lead them down a path of power strong enough to challenge us, it is our sworn duty to take action."

"Exactly," Veli said. "Well stated, Senator."

Frexle paused a moment to let the chatter die down. She was indeed correct. The purpose of the council was exactly as she had said, along with a smattering of other things such as voting on tax bills, pushing agendas, and managing the growth of the population in a strictly controlled fashion.

"You are, of course, correct in your assertion, Senator Kleeve," Frexle stated finally. "However, their argument is that we should target our efforts in such a way as to minimize damage."

"What does that mean?" Pookand asked.

"I'm completely lost," said Calloom.

"Well, sir," Frexle said, looking at the papers in front of him, "we currently have many methods under our employ. For example, we use massive asteroids to destroy entire planets."

"That's one of my top-five favorites," noted Veli.

Frexle bit his lip. "Worldwide plagues."

"Can get really creative with those," said Pookand.

"Infestations that destroy entire crops and cause mass famine," added Frexle.

"The invention of locusts was inspired," Kleeve said.

"It was nothing," Calloom replied humbly. "Just a stroke of luck."

"I could go on and on," Frexle said, looking up from his papers.

"Please do," Pookand requested.

"But the people are losing interest in these things," Frexle stated, ignoring Pookand. "What they're asking for is that we find a way to target our attacks and minimize the loss of life. The argument is that it makes no sense for a planet to be destroyed when we can simply sabotage or discredit the few individuals who are causing the changes in the first place. Their question, council members, is why do we need to engage in extermination?"

"It's fun?" suggested Pookand.

"It sates our bloodlust?" offered Kleeve.

"The kids love it?" Calloom noted.

Frexle held up the latest report from the polling booths. "The numbers I've brought today, senators, would suggest that the people are not as fond of it as they once were, and they're losing that fondness more and more as the days progress."

"Then let's set up a plan to hunt these dissenters down and kill them," Veli commanded.

"We could do that, Lord Overseer, but again we don't know precisely who they are."

"Shit," Veli said with a grunt. The familiar sound of tapping could be heard from his darkened archway. "Okay, Frexle, you've clearly thought about this. What do you suggest we do?"

Frexle took this moment to let it sink in with the rest of the senators that Lord Overseer Veli had just positioned him as an idea man. This meant a lot when dealing with the council because they were against change. Fortunately, they were more against being ousted or outright killed, and Veli was known to take drastic action against anyone who challenged his position. His world, after all, was a microcosm of the Overseers as a whole.

"As to that, Lord Overseer," Frexle began, "I have found a small ship with an unattached crew—"

"You mean there's nobody on the ship?" Calloom interrupted.

"No, Senator, I mean that the crew of this ship has no home world," Frexle replied. "Well, they obviously *came* from a planet, but these particular people have outgrown that planet and are no longer a part of it. They left it to live on their own."

"You mean they're starting a new world?"

"I don't think so, Senator Kleeve. They simply don't fit in

anymore. The planet that they come from is called Segnal." Frexle pulled up a visual and pointed to a small dot on the field of stars. "It is a bit slow, technologically."

"Are those ships on rails, Frexle?"

"Yes, Lord Overseer."

"That's the stupidest thing I've ever seen."

"And I would imagine that this small crew I'm speaking of would agree. You see, sir, the ship that they are flying in doesn't need rails. In fact, their ship has extremely advanced technology, including instantaneous travel, cloaking, and even time travel."

"Kill them at once!" shouted Veli.

"They must be destroyed," complained Pookand.

"They'll overrun us in no time!" Calloom argued with a shriek. "Think of the children, man!"

"I'll make posters straightaway," Kleeve chimed in.

"Wait, wait, wait," Frexle said a bit more loudly than he had intended. This garnered him harsh stares from the senators that he was able to see, and he could have sworn that he heard a growl from Veli's position. "I'm sorry to have raised my voice, esteemed council," he said with a quick bow of his head, "but you must understand that this tiny ship has no idea that we even exist. And even if they did, we are still more powerful than they are. Again, they're just a small crew." The silence was deafening. "Now, please don't get me wrong. My first thought was to destroy them with a massive bang, but then I got to thinking about the polling results and I wondered if maybe we couldn't utilize this ship as a tool to solve our issues."

"How do you mean?" said Veli after a time.

"Well, my lord, we could use them to do our dirty work for us."

"You mean espionage?" asked Pookand.

"Something like that, yes."

"That might work, actually," said Calloom. "Done right, we'd look like heroes to this *HadItWithTheKillings* group, too."

"Yes," said Veli, "but what about the assassinations and such? This crew you're suggesting would still manage things like that?"

"Statistically speaking, Lord Overseer, I can't imagine they'd be able to succeed without at least *some* measure of violence. But since their efforts would be on a smaller scale, it won't be as distasteful to those in our public who have lost their desire for blood."

"Hmmm," Veli said.

"Can we still have posters?" asked Kleeve.

"I'd say it's a must," answered Calloom.

"And," Pookand was quick to point out, "let's not forget about the golf on Landumbi."

"I wouldn't dream of forgetting that," Calloom said.

"Then it's settled?" said Frexle.

The room grew quiet as Veli thought things through. Everyone had said their piece and now it was up to the Lord Overseer to make the final determination. Frexle had done all he could to present his case. If Veli decided not to go with it, then the *HadItWithTheKillings* group would eventually take things over and install a new regime that carried its own problems. Until then, Frexle would continue doing his duty to the best of his ability.

"Fine," Veli said unhappily, "we'll give it a try, Frexle. If it fails, though, we will destroy this ship of yours, and then we'll go back to the killings as we've always done. Are we clear?"

"Yes, Lord Overseer."

"Where is this ship now?"

"In a mock battle that I set up, my lord," Frexle answered.

"I wanted to see how they would handle themselves in a state of conflict."

"Ooh," said Kleeve, again sitting forward, "I want to watch."

"Me too," agreed Pookand.

"Put it on-screen, Frexle," commanded Calloom.

GET US OUT OF HERE

*B*eing thrashed about in a spaceship isn't as fun as it sounds. Even the androids were starting to get into the swing of things as the unknown enemy upped their attack. Harr had never seen the *Reluctant* in such a state of disarray. Granted, it wasn't like she had been a sparkling new ship when he'd inherited her, and there was still a lot to her that he was unfamiliar with, but he was damn certain that the wires dangling from the ceiling hadn't been shooting sparks earlier that day.

Another hit caused the lights on the bridge to shut down.

"Geezer, the lights are out up here."

"Same down here, prime," Geezer replied. "Working on it."

"We still have control of the helm, thir."

"Good to know, Lieutenant."

"Weapons are still functioning," Curr added.

"Hitting anything?" asked Harr.

"Took out one of their smaller ships," said Middleton, "but there are still quite a few hot on our tail."

That's when it hit Harr. They didn't need rails to pull off

something like an Alpha-Theta-3-1-Switch. All they needed was the right mix of thrust, luck, and a complete disregard for physics. They'd survived on that concoction many times before.

"Geezer," Harr said excitedly, "remember when we were flying wildly toward that Kortnor space station during our first mission together?"

"Hard to forget, chief."

"Yeah, it truly was something."

"No, I mean it's hard for me to forget anything. I'm a robot, remember?"

"Right," Harr said with a grimace. "Point is that you had hooked up the *Reluctant* so we could use the thrusters to push us off course in a hurry."

"That was impressive, if I do say so myself. Completely impossible physics, that."

"True," Harr said, "but somehow you managed it."

"That's 'cause I was never any good at physics, honcho."

Harr laughed at that, but soon realized he was the only one who found it humorous. Chances are that not even Geezer had intended it as a joke.

"Incoming," said Jezden seconds before the *Reluctant* shuddered again. "Aft shields are down to ten percent. We can't take much more of this."

"You hear that, Geezer?"

"I *felt* it, big cat. I just don't know what to do about it."

"Well, can you manage to be equally poor at paying attention to the laws of the universe and find a way for us to outmaneuver these bastards?"

"Sure," Geezer said without hesitation. "Give me about an hour."

"You have two minutes."

"Seriously?" Geezer replied. "What is it with you starship captains? An engineer tells you that they need a certain amount of time to accomplish some ridiculous task, and you respond by giving them no time at all. How's that supposed to work?"

"Now's not the time—"

"But when I'm looking for my annual review," the irritated robot continued, "where are you to be found? Off drinking at some cantina, that's where.

"Honestly," Harr said as he sat in the dark, "I have no idea what you're talking about, but this just isn't—"

"And when I finally do manage to corner one of you higher-ups, I just hear some mumbo jumbo about how Human Resources has yet to get my paperwork back to you. So I ask when you expect to have everything in-hand and you give me a week as a timeframe. What would you say if I replied with, 'You've got two minutes?'"

"Geezer," Harr replied in a controlled tone, "this really isn't the time."

"Of course it isn't. When you're the one needing something, then it's all 'jump and run', but when a subordinate is in a hurry because he's made an unfortunate bet at the craps table on Soober-7 and he's in desperate need of that annual bonus because a certain mob boss has threatened to take away his favorite transistor and snip a couple of much needed wires, things can slow down to a snail's pace."

Harr's hands were starting to tire from gripping the edge of the armrests. Being unable to see much beyond the glow of the monitors made it even more trying to hold on when the ship rocked back and forth. If they did make it out of this alive, he was going to have to invest in some upgrades on his damn chair, and probably in better shields for the ship, too.

"Five percent," Jezden announced.

"Geezer," Harr barked, "I don't know where this is coming from, but if you don't give me the ability to steer this ship in whatever fashion I choose to within the next thirty seconds, you'll not live to worry about your annual bonus."

"Oh? Well, why didn't you say so, big cat? It's ready to go."

"Huh?"

"Do whatever you want with the engines," Geezer said. "They're ready."

"That fast?"

"I'm a robot, honcho. Multitasking is my middle name."

"According to your file," Sandoo said, "your middle name is Irving."

"That was supposed to be classified!"

"Can we get back to the problem at hand, please?" Harr yelled.

"Like I said, prime, I've already rigged up the engines and even had time to make a nice oil smoothie."

"That's swell," Harr replied, "but what are we supposed to do with the engines?"

"I thought you captains were supposed to know all this junk?" Geezer said after a moment. "Honestly amazes me how you rise up in rank the way you do. Just give it to one of the androids to manage it—except maybe Jezden, he'll just try to hump it."

Jezden said, "What?"

"Middleton," Harr commanded, "if I recall correctly, your record said that you were a hotshot on the race track back in Segnal."

"I didn't do too badly," Middleton replied. "Won my fair share, sir."

"Good. Take the controls and do whatever you have to in order to get us out of this mess."

"Roger that, sir. You all may want to hold on tight."

An instant later, the *Reluctant* whined and groaned as Middleton put her through the paces. Harr's stomach felt each drop, rise, twist, and turn as the ensign dodged missiles and laser fire. It didn't take long before the enemy could be seen on the main screen. Somehow Middleton had managed to do his own version of the Alpha-Theta-3-1-Switch.

"Can anyone target those ships?" Harr asked while fighting to keep his lunch down.

"Trying, sir," said Curr.

"I've got one of the smaller ones in my sights," announced Ridly. "Firing!" The beautiful vision of exploding metal filled the monitor as Ridly pumped her fist and said, "Yes!"

"Everyone target and fire at will," Harr commanded. "Geezer, take this time to get the GONE drive working."

"Yeah, yeah, I'm on it."

From there all hell broke loose. Lasers and missiles were being launched from the *Reluctant* left and right. The enemy was now on their heels, using evasive maneuvers as they were systematically hunted down and destroyed.

The lights came back on, shocking Harr's eyes and causing him to squint.

"Did we get them all?"

"No, thir," said Moon. "There are still a few more closing in."

"Two missiles incoming," Jezden said. "We're goners."

"Geezer?"

"Ready, honcho. Where to?"

"Away from here."

"Got any suggestions?"

"Now!"

"Fine!"

MEET THE NEW BOSS

*H*arr kept his eyes shut as the warm embrace of silence filled the air. No more explosions, no more rocking, no more thoughts of *Oh no, we're all gonna die!* Harr didn't know where they'd ended up, but with any luck it was better than the imminent destruction they had just escaped.

He pried his fingers from the armrest and began working them back into shape.

"Sir?"

"Give me a minute, Commander," Harr answered.

"I really think you should take a look at this, sir."

Harr sighed. Couldn't he have just a minute to recuperate? Just because they were androids didn't mean he was. They could process things in a split second and shut off their emotions even faster. Harr couldn't. He needed time to process and to calm down.

"Seriously, sir."

"Are we being shot at again, Commander?" Harr asked while rubbing his eyes.

"Well, no."

"Is there a giant space turtle about to mount our great ship?" he asked. It *had* happened before, after all.

"Not that I'm aware of, sir."

"Nope," ensign Curr said. "Just confirmed that there is no turtle humping us, sir."

"Has the self-destruct sequence on the *Reluctant* been activated and is just in a silent countdown?"

"I hope not," Sandoo said uncertainly.

"Then, what is so—" Harr opened his eyes and peered at the main view-screen to find that the ship was currently sitting inside of a massive containment system. It appeared similar to the old Segnal Outpost that housed half the SSMC fleet, only this one was easily ten times larger. "Where the hell are we?"

"It looks like a monster-sized landing bay, sir," suggested Middleton.

"Right."

Everyone moved to the screen and began looking around. The walls went up so far that they became so dim that the eye couldn't catch sight of the ceiling. He could tell that it was a circular building due to the slight angling of the walls all around. Looking down was a similar visual. The ship was being suspended in the middle of this monstrosity. What Harr didn't understand was *how*. He didn't see any beings in the gigantic room, nor were there other ships. At least nothing like the *Reluctant*.

A gentle cough sounded from behind them and they all spun back to see a middle-aged man with curly brown hair leaning against the back wall. He was roughly Harr's height and build, but his face didn't share Harr's superhero qualities. If anything, this guy's face was too lean to match his body. His eyes were definitely larger than what Harr would consider normal.

"Who the hell are you?" Harr asked, taking a step forward. "And how the hell did you get on my ship?"

"My name is Frexle," the man replied, "and I'm sorry to inform you that the *SSMC Reluctant* is not really your ship any longer, Captain Harr."

Sandoo reached for his sidearm, but Harr put out his hand to stop the android. If this Frexle character had the ability to transport sight unseen onto Harr's ship, it wasn't likely that a simple beam of energy would take him out. For all Harr knew, Frexle wasn't even physically aboard. It could just be a projection that they were seeing.

"A wise decision to stop good-old Commander Sandoo," Frexle said, clearly having more intel on the Platoon F crew than the Platoon F crew had on Frexle. "I would have hated to destroy you all on your first day under my employ."

"Wait, did you say that we're under your employ?"

"Correct, Captain," Frexle said with a tight smile. "You have come under the watchful eye of the Overseers. That's not a good thing, I assure you. Normally it results in immediate death, but we have a bit of a proposition that we thought you might like to hear."

"Propositions tend to put us in harm's way, Fractal."

"Frexle."

Harr ignored the correction. "We have a tendency of getting proposals that threaten to get us killed. Happens all the time."

"I see," Frexle said as he studied his fingernails. "Well, you can certainly bypass the proposition phase and just meet your demise immediately. Your choice, of course."

"I'm listening," Harr said with a sigh.

Frexle pushed off the back wall and walked awkwardly to Harr's chair. He sat down in it and crossed the thinnest set of legs Harr had ever seen. Frexle's feet were enormous, but the toothpicks that they were attached to couldn't have contained an ounce of fat.

"Captain, we have been on the lookout for a resourceful group that can take care of certain…items for us."

"What kind of items?"

"Oh," Frexle said, waving his arms, "just your basic things. Espionage, theft, assassinations, and other odd jobs."

"We're not killers."

"Kill or be killed, Captain, as the saying goes."

"Right," said Harr, weighing things. "Who are we killing, again?"

"If you're clever enough, possibly nobody." Frexle uncrossed his legs and then crossed them the other way. "But you must be *willing* to kill in the event that it becomes necessary."

"I see," Harr said, trying to buy time. If there was a way out of this, he'd have to find it fast. "Uh…who are these Overseers anyway?"

"We are the supreme intellect in the known universe."

"So there may be a smarter group in the unknown universe?" asked Harr.

"That's unknown."

"Right."

"Essentially, we are a collection of intelligent beings from various races and worlds that were hand-picked by the reigning Lord Overseer, Veli."

"And who is he, or is it a she?"

"Based on the timbre of voice," Frexle said as he wiggled his foot around, "I'd go with *he*, but I've never seen him. He sits in the shadows."

"Why?"

"Likely doesn't want his face to be known, but you'll find that a lot of species have their own set of peculiar quirks, so one can never be certain of their true motivations."

"Yes," Harr said with a nod, "I've learned that over the last couple of years. Anyway, if you guys are so smart, what do you need with us?"

"I've told you already, Captain."

"I'd like to understand the deeper meaning, Freckles."

"Frexle."

"You claim to be the most intelligent race in the universe, so why can't you take care of your own problems?"

"Okay, Captain," Frexle said with a look of surprise, "I guess the best way to answer that is to explain that when you've attained the level of greatness that we have, it's very easy to merely smite those deemed lesser if they get out of hand."

"I'm not sure I understand."

"How best to make this clear? Ah, yes. What's the main thing a person does when they get to the top of an organization?"

"Crap on everyone under them?" answered Harr.

"Fair enough," Frexle said with a nod. "What's another thing they do?"

"Start making insane rules?" suggested Middleton.

"Got me there, too," admitted Frexle. "The next thing, then?"

Curr raised his hand and said, "Change the direction of the organization toward a strategy previously employed while imagining—wrongly, by the way—that said strategy will suddenly work because *they* are in charge."

"Actually," Frexle said with a purse of his lips, "that happens also." He pushed himself up off the chair and somehow stayed balanced on those spindly legs. "Maybe I'll save us some time and just get to the point. What the aforementioned person does, folks, is fight to keep the position that they were finally able to attain."

"So you're saying that the Overseers spend the majority

of their time looking for civilizations that could possibly usurp them?"

"Not all of us, Captain Harr," Frexle replied, "but there is a division that is specifically assigned this task. Its job is to find potential threats, and then destroy them."

"What kind of threats are we talking here?" Harr asked.

"Any technological development that we feel may lead to advancements capable of challenging our level of sophistication."

"Sounds like you're talking about a Tower of Yebble," Harr noted.

"Sorry?"

"It's an old Segnalian story about how everyone got to building up this tower to reach the heavens. The gods didn't like it and thought that their creation was getting too powerful, so they spread the people out and changed their languages in an effort to slow them down."

"Interesting," Frexle said. "Did it work?"

"I doubt it's even true," Harr answered with a shrug. "But eventually Segnal ended up building rails that leave the planet and connected them to hubs and other planets along the way, so if the tower story is true, I'd wager that the splitting up of people ultimately failed."

"I see."

"What are some examples of technology that you kill people for?" Geezer asked through the comm.

"Ah," Frexle said with a grin as he pointed to the console on Harr's chair, "that's the robot, yes?" Harr nodded. "Well, let's see. A few examples would be faster-than-light travel, advanced computer systems, ability to control gravity, time travel, and fire."

"Fire?"

"Not *creating* it, Captain," Frexle said, "but rather, its discovery."

"As in rubbing sticks together?"

"Correct."

"How do you make the leap from discovering fire to challenging you for the top spot in the universe?"

Frexle pulled up his sleeve and tapped on his arm. An instant later, an image appeared on the *Reluctant's* main monitor. The visual showed a massive map of stars in one quadrant, a threat-level indicator in another, statistical analysis in another, and a series of graphs in the last one.

"This is a program written by the Lord Overseer. Its job is to take data from each culture on any given planet—everything from what they eat to where they shop, assuming they have evolved to the point of having places to shop—and extrapolate over the expected lifetime of the species how far they will grow. If the data suggests that they will expand to the point of being able to challenge us, we destroy them."

"You gotta realize that our ship has a few of those things you described," admitted Geezer. "Time travel, instant travel, and cloaking, at least."

"We are aware," said Frexle, "and typically having these items would result in your immediate destruction, but we're offering you a way to avoid that outcome."

"Wait a second here," Harr said, feeling worried. "You know about our particular advancements, but those are unique to us. Segnal doesn't have this level..."

"Since you've left, there's no reason to touch Segnal, Captain," Frexle said soothingly. "Our calculations show that you were an anomaly. Your world isn't likely to ever grow to anything useful. There was one piece of data that suggested Segnal would eventually be overrun by androids and then become a threat, but that somehow got removed from the timeline."

"Is that so?" Harr said with a cough as he glanced over at

Sandoo and shook his head. "Well, it seems you know a lot about us."

"As I said, Captain, we are the smartest race in the universe. We can see without being seen."

"Can you explain how you manage to do that?"

"Sure can't."

"Right," Harr said, not really expecting the answer anyway. "So you have all this capability and even a program that tells you who will potentially grow to be a threat, and yet you still haven't figured out a way to manage this little problem of yours?"

"Ah, but I have, Captain. I've found the *SSMC Reluctant.*" Frexle smiled proudly. "So, will you take the job?"

"It's not like we have much of a choice, Frexle."

"Frexle."

"That's what I said."

"Oh, yes, you did that time, didn't you?" Frexle blinked a few times. "Yes or no, Captain. Are you taking the job or not?"

"Again, what choice do we have?"

"So it's a yes, then?"

"Obviously it's a yes, you idiot," Jezden chimed in.

"Settle down, ensign," Harr said warningly.

Frexle stared over at Jezden for a few moments before saying, "Good."

"So what does this mean?" asked Harr.

"Training will begin soon," Frexle answered. "Be prepared." He paused and added, "Oh, and do note that we have installed a tracking device on your ship, so please don't get any ideas regarding escape. We will find you and the Overseers are not known for being forgiving."

And with that, he disappeared into the ether.

THAT WAS ODD

*D*id anyone else find that odd?" Harr asked as he thought things through. He looked up to see staring faces. "I mean, I know it's odd that some random person just showed up on the ship, and I know it's odd that we're in the hull of some massive hangar, and also that we've just been conscripted into service when we all thought for certain that we were finally free from that." He took a deep breath. "What I'm talking about is the absurdity that this supposedly uber-intelligent race needs us."

The *Reluctant* was still suffering from the beating she'd taken. Even though she was resting inside of the Overseer's landing bay, Harr could hear her distant groans. The ship wasn't sentient, of course, but as her captain, Harr felt what she felt. He had to. If he didn't, how could he properly guide her through the most challenging situations? Some captains claimed that when all was said and done, it was love that kept a ship going. Ensign Jezden would have said that was gay, but Harr couldn't help but think that all those captains were right.

"Thir," Lieutenant Moon said after a few moments, "it

seems to me that we don't have enough information about these people to know if it's strange or not."

Harr sat down in his chair and scratched his cheek. "We know that they consider themselves to be pretty smart," he said. "We know that they have the ability to transport onto our ship at will. We know..." He paused as a thought hit him. "Geezer, did you set the coordinates to this location when you activated the GONE drive?"

"Actually, chief, I don't even know where *here* is exactly. We're off the charts. I was trying to get us close to Fantasy Planet, thinking we could all do with a little R and R after that battle and all."

"Then, the GONE drive is malfunctioning?"

"Not as far as I can tell," Geezer answered, "but I'm not exactly an expert."

"You invented the damn thing, Geezer!"

"Through happenstance, honcho," Geezer corrected. "I just plug stuff in and stick wires here and there, and then I get lucky. You know that. I mean, sure, I can hook up thrusters and such like it's nobody's business, but time-travel devices, cloaking technology, and the GONE drive? Nah, that was pure luck."

"Wonderful."

"Crap," Geezer suddenly said. "I forgot I was on speaker."

"So?" Harr replied.

"So the entire crew just heard that, right?"

"Yes."

"Damn. Ah well, so much for them idolizing me."

"I don't think that was ever an issue," Harr said apologetically.

"Sir," Sandoo chimed in before Geezer could respond, "my guess is that these Overseers must have rescued us from that battle."

As if on cue, one of the panels erupted in flames. Curr

and Middleton struggled to snuff it out. Harr glanced around again and decided that he would have to get Frexle to fix up his ship, or give him and the Platoon F crew enough time to manage it themselves. Chances are they'd be doing it themselves.

"Or, Commander," Harr said seriously, "they were the ones who set up the battle in the first place."

"Why would they do that?"

Jezden grunted and said, "Probably to make sure we had the skill to fight."

"Agreed," Harr said. "And those ships *did* come out of nowhere."

"And they didn't even try to communicate with us," Moon stated.

"There was no backup, either," Curr noted as he sat back down. "No mother ship or anything."

"We don't have any mother ships on Segnal," Middleton pointed out, "so that's not much of an argument."

"Just because we don't doesn't mean that other worlds don't, Middleton."

"But you don't know if they do or not, Curr, which means you're just adding in nonsensical data to confuse the situation."

"How about if I stuff some nonsensical data up your—"

"Okay, you two," Harr said, raising his voice, "enough chatter. The point is that these guys obviously need *us*, and that makes me wonder how truly smart they are."

"Seeing that they overrode the GONE drive," Geezer said through the comm, "I'd say they're not idiots."

"Fair point."

"Sir," Sandoo said, "shouldn't we be focused on how to get out of this mess?"

"That's precisely what I'm doing, Commander. 'Know thy enemy,' as it were."

"Ah, yes. Well, in that case, Frexle did say we were going to be put through training. Maybe we can glean information about how they work then."

"Good thinking, Commander," Harr said. "Until then, let's get the *Reluctant* back in top shape. I have a feeling that Frexle's not going to lend us much help there."

BOOT CAMP

*I*t wasn't even two hours after the ship was back in shape before Frexle had delivered the entirety of Platoon F, including a very disgruntled Geezer—who had to bring a rolling tray with his battery affixed—to a planet called Sadian.

They were standing out in the desert in the middle of a compound that Harr could only assume served as a boot camp station.

As far as planets went, Sadian was like every other inhabitable planet he'd seen. Sky, dirt, wind, clouds, and while he couldn't see any, Harr was certain there were trees and areas of water somewhere in the distance.

Standing in front of him was a squat man who was built like a tank. He couldn't have been more than four feet tall. Sadian seemingly produced rather small humanoids, based on those present on the compound. Of course, it could just be that their military consisted of smaller races. That seemed out of place to Harr, but so did standing in the middle of a strange planet while getting ready to face yet another damn boot camp.

"My name is Drill Sergeant Razzin," the little drill instructor screamed in a controlled fashion, "and I have to say that you are the worst looking set of recruits I have ever seen. You are an embarrassment to this base and to the uniforms that you are wearing." Harr glanced around and noted that everyone still donned their standard-issue Segnal Space Marine Corps outfits. To be fair, even though the little soldier didn't know, Platoon F probably *would* be considered an embarrassment to the SSMC. "By hell," Razzin said, "there ain't a one of you under five feet tall! It's an atrocity. Makes a soldier wonder why they even let you land at this base." He paused and then pointed at the soldier next to him. "This is Corporal Woor, our regulations officer."

Razzin then motioned Woor forward. Woor was similar in size to Razzin, but he was not gruff-looking at all. In fact, he seemed rather pleasant.

"Regulation 7124B," Woor said in a complimentary tone of voice, "requires that I inform you that we actually think you all have super potential in your own way, and we can tell just by looking at you that you're all very nice people."

Razzin craned his head from side to side, clearly irritated that Woor was a part of this event. He then took a few steps forward and started sizing everyone up. There was something about a drill instructor that made a person uncomfortable, even if the top of said instructor's head only came up to your chest.

After walking up and down the line a few times, he stopped in front of Sandoo. "What's your name, boy?"

"Sandoo, Kip, sir!"

"And what do those stripes on your uniform set your rank as, Sandoo?"

"Commander, sir!"

"You don't look like you could command your way out of a latrine, Sandoo."

"No, sir!"

Razzin grunted and moved along to Lieutenant Moon.

Woor quickly stepped up to Sandoo and said, "As per regulation 1139, Commander Sandoo, it is my duty to inform you that we're positive you could manage your way successfully out of the most complicated of latrines."

"Thank you, sir!"

Razzin sighed heavily and glanced up at Moon. "What's your name?"

"Moon, Hank, thir! I'm a Lieutenant, thir!"

"I don't even know what a Lootantent is," Razzin said while pointing firmly at Moon, "but I'm assuming it's the lowest possible rank in your pathetic military because, by god, if it's not I will need to put serious thought as to how your world functions."

"Is that a sexist statement, thir?" Moon asked, almost threateningly.

"Of course it's a sexist statement, Moon," Razzin replied unfazed. "Everyone knows that this is a man's army, and you certainly do not look to be playing the part of a man."

"But I am a man, thir!"

"If you are a man, Moon, then I am a goddamn Farnoq beast."

"My body is female, thir, but my mind is all male."

Razzin stood there, dumbfounded. "I honestly don't even know what to say to that, Moon."

Woor, however, did. "Hello, Lootantent Moon—I hope I got that right. Well, according to regulation 6624C, we, in the Sadian military, think it's wonderful that you have volunteered to serve. We respect your choice to live as a man in a woman's body. Also, according to rider 1409 of the *Right to Equal Service Act*, we are pleased to extend a welcoming hand to all races, creeds, sexual preferences, and genders to the Sadian military. Except tallies...until now, apparently."

"Sorry, thir," Moon said. "Tallies?"

"Tall people," Woor answered with an apologetic smile.

"Oh," Moon said, and then asked, "Are there actually any females in the military? I don't see any."

"None, yet," admitted Woor, "though we have been trying for the past few years to get at least one of them to join up. It turns out that Sadian women find the concept of the Sadian military to be silly."

By now Razzin was standing in front of Harr. "And what's your story? You look like a damn superhero with that ridiculous chin of yours." Razzin moved his head this way and that, squinting up as if studying. "If I didn't know any better, I'd wager that you had some kind of physical alterations done, son. Then again, looking at your Lootantent Moon over here, who knows what in blazes happens on your backward planet."

"Harr, Don, Captain of the *SSMC Reluctant*...sir."

"So, you're this group's leader, eh?" Harr kept his eyes straight ahead. "You must think you're some kind of hotshot, then."

"I'm a captain by vote, sir. We are no longer part of the Segnal military."

"That's right, you're not," Razzin affirmed tightly. "You're now part of the Sadian military, and that means—" Another Sadian soldier shuffled up and whispered into Razzin's ear. "Oh, right, I mean that you're now a part of the Overseer's Special Forces group." He stopped and turned back to the soldier. "They have special ops now?" More whispering. "Huh, well, okay, then. That changes things a bit." The whispering soldier scuttled away and Razzin turned back to face Harr. "I'm assuming you've already had basic training on this planet of yours?"

"We have."

"We have, *sir*."

Harr fought to maintain his composure. "We have, sir."

"So you know hand-to-hand combat already?"

"We were trained in hand-to-hand combat, sir."

"I'll bet you think you could take me in a fight, don't you, Captain? You're all tall and big and have a swagger about you. No doubt you think that we're just wee folk who couldn't handle someone of your size. Isn't that right, Harr?"

"Probably, sir."

"Well, I'll make a little deal with you, then," Razzin stated with a poke to Harr's chest. "If you or any of your soldiers can take me in the ring, I'll go easy on you. Hell, I'll even respect your previous training and move you right past the physical and on to the clerical. If you lose, though, you'll be going through boot camp all over again, Sadian style."

"You'll fight any of us?" Harr asked, purposefully leaving off the "sir."

"Actually, I'll fight all of you—one after the other, Captain. You'll find that I'm a tireless fighter."

"Excellent," said Harr, making eye contact. "When do we start?"

THE FIGHT

The walk across the compound brought smells of freshly baked bread, something that simultaneously seemed odd to Harr and caused him to feel hungry. He'd not had a decent meal in quite a while. Protein bars were somewhat tasty, but a home-cooked meal was a distant memory. The very fact that he just had cravings for boot camp food was a testament to the fact that protein bars can only take the palate so far.

Geezer was getting a stern talking to by one of the secondary drill instructors the entire way.

"Move your feet, mister!"

"I'm trying, buddy."

"Don't you call me that, soldier. I'm a *sir* to you."

"Sorry, pal. Still getting used to all of this."

"Sorry, *sir*!"

"It's okay," Geezer replied. "I know you're just doing your job."

"What? No, I mean you are to call me *sir*, like I said before."

"Oh, right. Gotcha. It's just not in my programming to do that. Hard thing to change...uh...sir."

Harr sniffed as a small smile crept to his lips. That turned into a full-on grin when Woor spoke next.

"You're doing wonderfully, soldier," he said to Geezer. "In fact, according to regulation 4535, you may even receive an award for effort."

"No foolin'?" said Geezer.

"No fooling, soldier. We, in the Sadian military, believe that everyone deserves to win, regardless of their skill level. It's called a participation medal. There are many of them."

"Come on," Geezer said. "You're shitting me, right?"

"We in the Sadian military make every effort to not defecate on anyone, soldier," Woor said seriously, "though regulation 9883, subsection 73-A does allow for it in the event that a particular soldier suffers from incontinence. I, however, do not suffer from said condition, which therefore means that I am in no way shitting you."

They approached a tent that sat just beyond the main barracks. Tension wires held down the green tarp edges by connecting to rings of metal that stuck out of the ground. Everyone had to duck in order to get inside. Everyone except for the Sadians, of course.

Once inside, Harr noticed the familiar image of a boxing ring. It was nearly identical to the ones on Segnal. Three ropes wrapped around a square platform with steps going up on opposing corners. A small table with three chairs sat on the side. It contained a little bell that Harr guessed was used to begin a round. There was even a microphone dangling from a cord that was affixed to the apex of the tent. The only difference that Harr could make out was the size of the ring. It was about half of what Harr was used to seeing. Then again, so were the Sadians.

"Okay," said Razzin, puffing his chest out, "who wants to fight me first?"

"I will," Harr replied, anxious to knock the little twerp into next week.

"Good," Razzin said with a sneer. Then he clapped his hands and yelled, "We've got a fight on!"

A loud bell rang across the compound and within minutes the room was awash with Sadian soldiers. Some were climbing up into the bleachers, hunting for a good seat. Others ran from station to station, putting on vendor outfits, heating up popcorn and hot dogs, and even offering up what appeared to be posters and T-shirts of Razzin. Clearly, the man had a reputation. Maybe there was something to the fellow that Harr had underestimated.

A Sadian with a snarly grimace started tugging Harr by the arm, doing his best to drag the captain to the challenger's corner. His one eye was squinting and he held a pipe in his teeth. The set of rough whiskers that adorned his chin served to give him that rugged appearance of a man who'd seen action.

"Name?" he said as a smaller, more serious-looking Sadian set about putting boxing gloves on Harr.

"Harr, Don."

"Captain?"

"Yes."

"Okay, 'Captain Harr Don' it is. Height?"

"No, wait. Say it like 'Captain Harr, first name is Don' and that way it won't sound—"

"Height?"

Harr sighed. "Around six feet."

"Unfortunate. Weight?"

"Two hundred and twenty pounds, last checked."

"That's a lot."

"I could stand to lose a few," admitted Harr.

"Professional record?"

"For boxing?"

"No," the man replied with a fixed stare, "for flower-bouquet decorating prowess. Yes, for boxing."

"I'm not a professional, so—"

"Zero and zero, then. Clean slate. Too bad it'll be zero and one by the end of the first round."

"He's that good, is he?"

"The best. Undefeated in nearly two hundred bouts."

"Any suggestions?" asked Harr.

"Run?"

The man walked over to the little table and handed the form he'd been working on to a Sadian who was wearing a tuxedo. These people really took their boxing seriously.

After multiple attempts, they finally found a pair of gloves that would fit Harr, but even the ones they settled on were quite snug. That's when the man who had taken his details came back.

"Name's Ugger," he said. "I'm in your corner along with Coobs here. Give me a quick rundown on what we're working with. You got any formal training?"

"Just boot camp hand-to-hand combat tactics from my home world of Segnal," Harr answered.

"Been in a ring before?"

"A couple of times."

"Know what a left hook is?"

"Of course."

"Right hook?"

"Same as the left, but from the opposite side?" Harr answered with a heavy dose of snark.

"Uppercut?"

"Yes."

"Good, good. You can't use any of those. They're not allowed."

"What?"

"Only jabs are allowed in a real-man's boxing match."

"Uh…" Harr replied with a squint.

"Ever knocked anyone out in the ring?" Ugger continued his questioning.

"Not with a jab," Harr answered, and then added, "Look, I told you already, I'm not a professional."

"All right, all right," Ugger said, "just calm down. Now, here's what we're going to do. You'll go in and make a show of it, see? Dance around a little, take a few jabs, that kind of thing. As soon as Razzin lands the first punch, you fall down, and I'll throw in the towel."

"What?"

"It's the best strategy."

"I'm not taking a dive," Harr said with a frown.

Ding ding ding!

"Your call, buddy," Ugger said. "Any next of kin I should notify?"

Gentlemen and, well, other gentlemen, it's about tooooooooooooooo happennnnnnnnnnnnn!

(cheers)

Live from the Sadian Barracks in West Yalps, we present the fight of the night...or afternoon, as the case may be.

(cheers)

In this corner, standing roughly six feet tall and weighing in around two hundred pounds, with a record of zero and zero, coming to you from the planet of Segnal as part of the Segnal Space Marine Corps, the challenger, Captain Harrrrrrrr Donnnnnnnn!

(laughter)

And in this corner, standing four feet, one inch, and weighing in at seventy-seven pounds, with a record of one hundred ninety-seven wins and zero losses, originally from the eastern part of

Bladinger Heights, the reigning Champion of the World...Reldo "The Wrecker" Razzin!

(cheers and whistles)

Your referee for this bout is Axen Rems.

(mild, sporadic clapping)

"All right," the ref said, "bring it in. I want a clean fight. When I say 'break,' you break. Obey my commands at all times. Any questions?" Both fighters shook their heads. "Back to your corners."

"Last chance, pal," Ugger said.

"I'm not taking a dive."

"I'll keep the towel handy in case you change your mind."

The bell rang and Harr came out to the center of the ring with his hands up to protect his chin. He quickly adjusted them lower, seeing as there was little chance that Razzin could reach his chin.

Razzin's footwork was impressive. He hopped from left to right with the grace of a deer in a meadow, but when he reached out for a quick jab, the distance his hand traveled was so short that Harr didn't even have to move.

Then, with a burst of speed, Razzin came in with his fists flying. Harr instinctively reached out and put his hand on Razzin's head, keeping the man at bay as his tiny arms blurred in a swarm of speedy punches.

The ref slapped Harr's hand away, but Harr put it right back. The ref slapped it away again. Harr put it back again. This happened repeatedly until the ref yelled, "Time." He then instructed Razzin to take his corner and he pushed Harr over to his. "You can't put your hand on his head."

"Why not?"

"Because it's in the rules."

"Oh," said Harr. "Well, what else can't I do, then?"

"You mean you don't know the rules?"

"Apparently not for your brand of boxing."

"Fine," the ref said. "No kicking, biting, spitting, kneeing, throwing, name-calling or putting your hand on your opponent's head to keep him at bay."

"So, we can only throw punches?"

"Well, you can block them too."

"Right."

The ref jumped out into the middle of the ring and made a cutting motion with his hand to signify it was time for the fighters to resume.

Harr took the center of the ring as quickly as possible. Razzin zipped in and threw a number of jabs. None of them connected. The speed that the little fellow moved made it difficult for Harr to get a lock on his head, but soon a pattern emerged. Two hops left, one right, jab. One left, one right, two jabs. One left, two right, jab.

Harr let the rhythm sink in while readying his onslaught, and then unleashed a straight punch that caught Razzin square in the kisser, knocking him off his feet and landing him flat on his back, unmoving.

The crowd silenced.

"Huh," Harr said while standing over the fallen Razzin. "That was easier than expected."

Ref Rems stood for a moment in shocked silence, but soon remembered his duty and started the count. Once he hit ten, he waved his arms and the crowd cheered louder than before. They had a new champion.

Your winner, by way of knockout, and newwwwwwwwwwww Champion of the World...Captain Harr Don!

The cheers were deafening as Harr left the ring, leaving a beaten Razzin to the care of physicians.

Little hands slapped him on his lower back as he exited the building. Ugger was in tow, offering to be his manager. As he passed one of the kiosks, he noted an exceptionally entrepreneurial Sadian who was already making "Captain Harr Don" T-shirts available for order.

PAPERWORK

The next morning, Drill Sergeant Razzin was even more obstinate than he'd been the day before. Obviously, he was a sore loser. It probably didn't help that his left eye was all but swollen shut. Harr felt oddly good about that.

"The real fun is about to begin, soldiers," Razzin said. "You'll have to work your tails off if you're to earn the right to be in this man's army."

"And, per regulation 2299G," noted Woor, "woman's army, even if there aren't any yet."

"Now, drop and give me twenty!"

"Wait a second, here, Razzin," Harr said, stepping forward and causing Razzin to get into a fighting stance.

"Watch yourself, mister."

"I don't want to fight you again," Harr said with a grimace. "Wasn't much of a fight anyway."

"Oh yeah?"

"Look, we had a deal. You said if any one of us beat you in the ring, boot camp was going to be lax on the physical. If you don't uphold your end of the bargain, you'll have zero respect from my crew."

"So, that's how it works on Segnal, eh?" Razzin said, lowering his fists. "You make a bet and welsh on the outcome and you're considered slimy for that?"

"Pretty much, yes," Harr replied. "Actually, I'd argue that's true on every planet."

"Well, not on Sadian, mister. We welsh on bets all the time here. If we didn't, we'd all be broke!"

"Not all of you," noted Harr. "That would be impossible. Someone has to win those bets, obviously."

"Enough talk," Razzin commanded in a voice that meant business. "Drop and give me twenty."

Harr stood tall and crossed his arms defiantly.

"Did you not hear me, Harr?"

"I heard you just fine," Harr said. "I'm just not going to comply."

"Is that so? Well, let's just see how tough you are when I put a little squeeze on your team." He turned to the rest of the squad, who had by now hopped back to their feet. "It seems that your captain, here, thinks he's above doing the things that a recruit is expected to do. Since that's the case, all of *you* are going to pick up his slack! Now, drop and give me a hundred!"

Again, they all dropped and started doing push-ups. Harr just glowered at Razzin and smiled in a not-so-friendly way.

The little man *was* employing the correct tactic. Make all the others do extra work so that the one slacker ended up in their crosshairs. Eventually that slacker would be the hardest-working bastard in the bunch, after he'd healed from the beatings, of course. But, obviously, Razzin hadn't gotten the memo about Platoon F being full of androids.

"It looks like your metal-man feels he's above being a soldier too, eh?"

"Nope, chief," Geezer replied before Harr could. "I just can't physically do a push-up."

Razzin glanced at Harr. "Is that true?"

"It's true. Look at his body shape and his arms. Frankly, he shouldn't even be out here. His battery isn't going to last forever."

"What's he good for, then?"

"He's the ship's engineer," Harr answered. "He keeps the ship running. You can tell by looking at him that he wasn't built for fighting, jogging, sprinting, or any other demanding physical activity."

"Then why did you bring him down here?"

"Following orders...sir."

"Oh, I see how it is," said Razzin while taking a step backward and throwing his arms up. "You're one of those types who follows orders when it's convenient." He turned to the crew. "Drop and give me another hundred." They dropped and started pumping their arms without hesitation. Razzin walked up and down the line and saw that the soldiers weren't tired in the least. "They're a resilient bunch," he said when he'd returned to Harr.

"Yep," agreed Harr. "You can do whatever you want to them. They're not going to tire out."

"We'll see about that," Razzin said in challenge. "They're about to go on a ten-mile run."

"Make it twenty," Harr replied. "They don't care."

"I'll make it fifty!"

"They won't even break a sweat."

"You're pretty damned confident in your soldiers, Captain."

"Supremely...sir."

That stopped Razzin in his tracks. He stared up at Harr for a few moments before he slowly started to nod. Then he squinted and studied back over the rest of the bunch, stopping to scoff at Geezer.

Harr felt bad for faulting the man. He was only doing his job. It wasn't easy being a drill instructor. Sure, you got to yell at people all day, and you got to inflict all sorts of punishments simply because you'd had a bad morning, but deep down you knew the recruits hated your guts. Eventually, assuming you did your job right, they'd learn to respect you. Hell, they'd eventually thank the stars you were there to whip them into shape should an actual battle ever come to their doorstep. Until then, though, you *were* the enemy.

"I hate to say it," Razzin said quietly, "but I admire that in a leader. It's a shame that they're going to hate you after I put them through the wringer."

The androids did their final twenty push-ups and then stood in unison. None of them were breathing heavily and there wasn't a bead of sweat to be found.

"Huh. That's odd. It's like they haven't stressed themselves in the least."

"Told you."

"Well," Razzin said, putting his hands on his hips, "if I have no leverage on you or your squad, why the hell are you here?"

"Frexle told us to be here," Harr answered. "Frankly, I'm not sure what it is you're supposed to be teaching us. We can obviously outdo you in physical tests, and at hand-to-hand combat you were no match for me—no offense. What else is there that you could possibly excel at that we don't?"

Razzin snapped his fingers and pointed at Harr. "Paperwork."

"What?"

"The Overseers love paperwork, which is how we became part of their clique in the first place." Razzin had the look of a man who'd struck gold. "Reports, updates, spreadsheets, presentations, and things of that nature. Reams and reams of paper filled with all variants of statistical analysis. They love it. We're good at it. That's what you're going to learn."

Harr felt a tightness in his chest. "Actually," he said with a gulp, "maybe those push-ups aren't such a bad idea after all."

THE UPDATE

he only thing worse than standing in front of the senate was having a one-on-one with Veli. There was something intimidating enough about the Lord Overseer that made Frexle fight to keep his blood pressure under control. It probably had to do with the fact that Veli was ever in the shadows. No, that couldn't be it. He'd been summoned to numerous meetings with council officials and senators who kept themselves as secretive as Veli. Whatever it was that was different about Veli, it served to keep Frexle on his toes.

"How's this crew of yours doing?" Veli said between what Frexle assumed were chews, since there was a grating sound of loud crunches, and it was dinnertime.

"Razzin says that they were incredibly adept at both the physical work and the paperwork, my lord. All except for their captain, anyway."

"Oh?"

"It seems that he was incapable of competing with his crew in the number-crunching arena. Razzin remarked that all but Harr were insanely fast at running reports."

"Shows that their captain is the real brains," Veli pointed out.

"Sorry, sir?"

"Think about it, Frexle," Veli said after a crunch and what sounded like a cut-off cry. "He can probably outdo anyone on his crew. But to do that would mean he'd be on their level, so he did what any wise leader would do: very little."

"That does seem to be the case with leaders," Frexle said without thinking.

"Watch yourself, Frexle."

"Present company excluded, of course, Lord Overseer."

"Of course," Veli said as a little creature ran across his desk. A black whip flew out and snapped it right back into the shadows with a squeal. "What's the next step?"

Frexle gulped. "Get them out into the field, my lord."

"Good. The planet of Kallian has made too many strides as it is. They're only a couple of days away from testing their warp technology. If that test succeeds, you know what happens?"

"Faster-than-light travel?"

"Besides that."

"Annihilation of their species," Frexle stated softly.

"Everyone on the senate knows that this is the only possible outcome, but we're following your lead on this, Frexle. If this Platoon F of yours succeeds with their mission and our popularity rating continues to drop while the *HadItWithTheKillings* group rises, you and I are going to have a very short talk."

"You mean a long talk, my lord?"

"No, a short one." There was another crunch. "It doesn't take much talk to kill you. For example, I'll say something like, 'Now you die,' and then I will kill you. See? Short talk."

"But, my lord, you must see that I'm just the messenger in

all of this? I brought you the reports and offered a possible solution, nothing more."

"Poor Frexle," Veli said with a chuckle. "Haven't you heard the old saying that you always kill the messenger?"

"With all due respect, Lord Overseer, I believe the saying is, 'Don't kill the messenger.'"

"Maybe where you come from," Veli replied after another crunch.

CREW MEETING

*A*ndroids or not, everyone on the *Reluctant's* bridge was beat. Harr didn't know if it was part of their programming to show fatigue after a while or if working with spreadsheets affected all races the same way, even digital ones. This was a first where he was the least fatigued person on the ship. Mostly because he'd acted in a supervisory role on Sadian.

Android software had built-in curiosity and emotion, and they were developed to be as close to human as possible, so much so that it had taken Harr half of their first mission together to realize that they were androids. Because of this, Harr made it a point to treat them like he'd treat any human soldier.

"Listen up," he said from his chair. Sandoo stoically stood. "Sit back down, Commander. Be at ease." Sandoo complied. "Okay, people, I know about as much as you do regarding the plan for this crew; but, whatever happens, just remember that my top priority is to keep you all safe."

Half of them seemed to relax a bit at his statement. Their programming was incredible. Lieutenant Moon was even rubbing his temples. It was almost a shame that there wasn't any booze on board because this bunch could have done with a stiff drink at the moment, although it probably wouldn't have had any actual effect on them.

"No offense, captain," Jezden said, his feet up on one of the consoles, "but I doubt you could hook up two hundred push-ups, and for us it was nothing."

"Your point?"

"Just that I'm not sure you'd be any better at protecting us than we'd be at protecting ourselves."

"I'll admit that you are all physically stronger than me," Harr said.

"And faster," Curr said.

"And smarter," Middleton pointed out.

"And less prone to injury," Jezden noted.

"And—"

"Enough," Harr said and then pushed himself up from his chair. "I get it, already. Yes, all of those things are true. Each of you can outperform me on basically every conceivable test. But that begs the question of why you asked me to remain in charge?"

"Because you're the most qualified, sir," Sandoo said.

"In what way, specifically, Commander?"

"Yeah," Jezden said, "how?"

"He thinks outside of the box," Sandoo replied matter-of-factly.

"Precisely," Harr said with a smile. "That's not a slight on any of you at all. You weren't programmed that way. You're hemmed in to a particular pattern of thought. In those specific areas, you're fantastic, and I would wager that the majority of humans would give up a lot to be able to focus and succeed the way that you can. Your sights are laser-guided. You see a hole and you fill it."

"That's true," Jezden agreed.

Harr scratched his chin. "But you still see things in a very linear fashion. You can't wriggle out of bad situations the way I can. Your survival instinct, while strong, is infinitesimal compared to mine."

"Or mine," Geezer chimed in over the com.

"True," Harr said with a nod. "Geezer's is probably more powerful than all of ours combined."

"Thanks, chief."

Harr was pacing back and forth now, using hand gestures and everything. "So, while you can all certainly do better than me in known situations that require speed, agility, and number-crunching, I can weasel my way through trials that would cripple your logic circuits."

At this point they were all nodding.

He took this time to glance around his ship. *Their* ship. The crew had patched her up so well that she was as good as —if not better than—when he'd first stepped aboard. There were still a few burn marks on the panels that had caught on fire, but that only served to bring more character to her.

"That, folks," Harr added, "is why you asked me to remain as captain of this vessel. And I take your faith in me seriously, which is why, again, I will do my best to use the conniving skills that we humans are ingrained with to protect you to my fullest ability. All I ask in return is that you watch and learn because I'm not going to be here forever."

Jezden leaned back, sighed, and said, "Gay."

VOOL

*F*rexle was in the midst of a late dinner when an underling approached and informed him that the Lord Overseer wished to see him again. He'd just left the man's office not an hour ago, but when the boss calls, you go. He dropped his head and brought his tray to the recycling line while chewing his last bite of stringy beef. A couple quick sips of water helped wash everything down as he walked the corridor back toward Veli's wing.

The *click clack* of his shoes on the marble floor echoed down the hallway, reminding him that it was late. Everyone had already gone home for the evening. This was usually the time he'd get to spend catching up on paperwork, of which there were mountains. Sometimes one of the senators stayed late and assumed Frexle had stuck around in case they needed him. More often than not, they were correct. Frexle wasn't a fan of senators doing anything unsupervised. But it was a rare thing for the Lord Overseer to stay beyond normal hours. Or, if he did, he certainly didn't tell anyone about it.

Frexle rounded the final turn and took a deep breath

before knocking on the door.

"Yeah."

He stepped inside and moved to a position behind the two chairs that sat before Veli's enormous desk. As always, Veli could not be seen.

"Sit down, Frexle."

"As you wish, Lord Overseer."

"I've been thinking about things since you left," Veli said in a tight voice. Frexle glanced to the right and noticed a pile of bones that marked the remains of Veli's dinner. "I've come to the conclusion that I don't like leaving things to chance."

"Sir?"

"Regardless of what this *HadItWithTheKillings* group wants from us, we still have a job to do, and I want to ensure it gets done correctly."

"I understand, my lord," said Frexle, biting his tongue. "May I ask what you had in mind, sir?"

There was a buzzing sound from Veli's desk. "Send her in."

Frexle turned to see a humanoid female walking in through the secondary entrance. Not very many people were allowed through that door, either in or out. Definitely not Frexle.

He recognized her face at once. It was hard to miss, as was the rest of her. Long blond hair, stunning purple eyes, and a body to die for. That was fitting since that was precisely what she was known for: killing. There wasn't a person in the upper echelons of government who hadn't utilized her skills at one time or another. She had no fear. She had no conscience. Or, if she did, she was damn good at hiding it. Worst of all, though, she was blunt.

"Vool, sir?" Frexle said with a concerned look on his face.

"Is that a problem, Frexle?"

"Well, my lord, it's just that she's..." Frexle paused,

recognizing the irony of what he was about to say, "not very tactful."

"Stuff it, Frexle," Vool said before plopping down in the chair next to him.

"See?"

"She'll do fine," Veli said, sounding less than convinced, himself. "Besides, she's not afraid to do what needs doing in the event that things need to get done."

"Huh?"

"Forget it," Veli grumbled. "Vool, I expect you to be on your best behavior."

"Whatever."

"You won't kill unless instructed to do so."

"Yeah, yeah, yeah."

"You will be reporting to this Captain Harr Don fellow," Veli continued, his voice grating more and more with each sentence.

"Captain Hard-on?" Vool said. "Like him already." She looked at her nails and furrowed her brow. Then she bit what appeared to be a hangnail before looking back up. "So, same job as always, right? I kill everyone on board this stupid ship and then we blow up some planet."

"No," Veli said tersely. "That's not even remotely what I just said, Vool. Now, pay attention. You are *not* to kill anyone unless expressly instructed to do so. Are we clear?"

"If I'm not killing anyone, why am I here?"

"Because it may come to a point where we *want* you to kill someone," Veli explained.

"Sir," Frexle said in a moment of inspiration, "I could go with the Platoon F crew and watch over things."

"I've already thought of that, Frexle. The problem is that you've got a conscience. Everyone knows it. Some members of the executive council even think you've lost your stomach for killing."

"Who?" said Frexle while rising in his seat.

"Me, for one," Veli replied directly.

Frexle slouched back down. "Oh."

"Vool," Veli said, "again, you'll do this job and do it right. No killings unless *I* say so, and *only* if I say so. There will be *no* mistakes about this."

Vool just rolled her eyes and refocused on her nails. How she was still living after treating the Lord Overseer as such, Frexle couldn't say. The first thought was that she was a daughter of Senator Menlorze, but the more likely answer was that she was good at what she did.

"This new crew that Frexle has put together is going to try for a—it pains me to say this—diplomatic resolution."

"That sounds horrible."

"I agree, but according to Frexle, the people are starting to feel that we're nothing but a murderous bunch of monsters."

"What's wrong with that?"

"Nothing, from where I sit," Veli said, "but politics are what they are. We have to put on a gentler, more understanding face for a little while."

"Damn liberals," said Vool.

"That's what I said," Veli agreed.

"Why don't we just kill them, too?"

"I suggested that as well," answered Veli in a defeated tone. "It turns out that *they* aren't easy to track. It's mostly just an idea that's taking storm among the populace."

"Ideas are stupid," Vool said.

"Right, well, speaking of ideas," Veli started, "I want you to do something else for me before you destroy Frexle's crew."

"You mean if they don't succeed—right, Lord Overseer?"

"What's that? Oh, yeah, sure, right. Frexle's right." Veli coughed. "Only if they don't succeed."

"What do you want?" Vool asked.

"I want you to find out where they got all that technology on their ship."

"What technology?" Vool asked with a tilt of her head.

"They have instantaneous travel, cloaking, and time travel," explained Veli.

"Shouldn't we kill them immediately?" asked Vool as if it weren't nearly as dire an issue from her perspective as it had been to the council.

"Yes, but again, we're not going to. Just find out about the technology."

Frexle sat forward. "We could just ask them, my lord?"

"Ask them what?"

"About their technology."

"Honestly, Frexle," Veli said with a huff, "sometimes you are exceedingly naive. People are very close-mouthed with their information. You could put thumbscrews to those people—which you should certainly try, Vool, assuming the mission is a failure and all—and they wouldn't tell you a thing. And even if they did tell you, it would be a lie."

"They seemed pretty forthright to me, my lord."

"I'm sure they are," Veli said, "about things such as the types of food they like, the kind of movies they watch, and their favorite places to shop, but we're talking about military things here."

"But they're in our military now, sir."

"Exactly," Veli said loudly, "and that's why I want to know where they got that technology."

"I—" Frexle stopped himself. There was really no point continuing the argument. It didn't matter what he said at this point. Veli's mind was made up. "We'll do it your way, of course, Lord Overseer."

"Yes," Veli said, "we will."

MISSION DETAILS

*A*t the core, it was probably a good thing that these Overseers had appeared when they did. The reality was that running a crew without any real goals or purpose is quite a challenge. Harr had spent a lot of time after leaving Segnal trying to figure out what exactly the crew was going to do. He'd considered becoming traders, hopping from world to world, bringing new and exciting technologies and foodstuffs and creatures, but then realized that he'd not only be messing with societal infrastructures, he'd also be introducing new bacteria and viruses. He'd had no interest in playing god. There was always the possibility of finding a grouping of worlds that had caught up with each other's technology, or maybe there was a system where explorers had branched out from their originating planet and kept the supply chains going. With his troop of androids and his advanced technology, he could only imagine that the *Reluctant* would be highly competitive wherever they set up shop.

Now, though, they were part of a new military, awaiting new orders. Part of him wanted to rebel against this, seeing that he'd just left this party, but another part of him liked the structure of things. Fact was that while he felt that he was growing into the leadership role that was dumped on him, he still preferred having someone above him who kept the missions coming. Wriggling out of situations was in his DNA; coming up with situations to wriggle out of, was not.

So when Frexle showed up on the bridge and slipped into the command chair, Harr had to admit that he'd felt a bit of relief. And now that Frexle was again sitting in that chair, detailing the upcoming mission, Platoon F's sense of structure was reengaged.

Harr's only concern was the person whom Frexle had brought along with him. She seemed cold and callous, not to mention seriously lacking when it came to tact. The only person on the *Reluctant* who found her interesting, of course, was Jezden.

"The world is called Kallian," Frexle said while displaying a floating, three-dimensional map. "It's in the Nebemus sector, at least according to your computer's files. We have it listed in the Carbellis sector, but we didn't want to confuse you." Nobody replied. "You're welcome." Again, no reply. "Well, anyway, the Kallians are in the process of developing warp technology. We need that stopped."

"Sorry to interrupt," Harr said, "but what is warp technology?"

"You can't be serious, Captain. Your ship has instantaneous travel and you don't know what warp technology is?"

"I sure don't."

"Fascinating."

Geezer, who had come up the lift to be part of the meeting, said, "Are you talking about that space bubble stuff from those TV shows years back?"

"Space bubble?"

"Honestly," said Vool with a sigh, "we should just kill them all now."

"What?" said Harr.

"She's kidding," Frexle said tersely, giving Vool a sharp look.

"No, I'm—"

"Anyway," Frexle interrupted, and then brought up an image of a ship zooming through space, "warp gets its name from the concept of warping space around an entity. It allows for velocities that are faster than the speed of light, but it does so without greatly impacting time dilation."

"Yeah," Geezer said. "Space bubble. Same thing, different name."

"Good," Frexle said, returning to the map view. "Now that we have a point of reference, we need you to stop the Kallians from succeeding with this technology. If they are successful, they will be deemed a serious threat, and that means their world needs to be destroyed."

"So you want us to sabotage their test."

"Correct, Captain. Get in and blow up the place, or do whatever you have to do. Just make sure it fails."

"I don't like the concept of killing innocents, Frexle."

"The needs of the many outweigh the needs of the few, Captain."

"Hey," Geezer said, "that's a line from the TV show that had space-bubble technology."

"Really?"

"Yeah. The show was called *Stellar Hike*. Maybe you've heard of it?"

Frexle seemed to be searching his memory, but eventually he shrugged. "Sorry, no, but I'll be sure to look it up. Always in search of a decent show to watch." He turned back to Harr. "Are we clear on what needs to be done, Captain?"

"Seems straightforward enough," Harr replied.

"Excellent," Frexle said with a clap of his hands. "Now, since this is your first mission, the Overseers have elected to send along one of our operatives."

"I assume you mean her?" Commander Sandoo asked without a trace of malice.

"Aren't you astute?" Vool rolled her eyes.

"Yes," Frexle answered Sandoo. "Vool will be taking notes on the things you do. However, Captain, you are still in charge of this mission. We're not here to interfere, but rather to judge."

"Thir," asked Lieutenant Moon, "if we are unable to stop the Kallians from thucktheeding, what will happen to them?"

Frexle evaluated Moon for a few moments before saying, "I'm sorry, but what do you mean by thucktheeding?"

"Um, you know, thir, if they're thuckthethful."

"Thuckthethful?"

Harr stepped in and said, "He's asking what happens if we can't stop the Kallians from making their technology work?"

"He?"

"Long story."

"Right," Frexle said, looking Harr over once more before continuing on. "What will happen is that we'll destroy Kallian and all of its inhabitants."

"And then," added Vool, "we'll kill all of you."

"What?"

"Sadly, she's correct. Failure is not an option, Captain. Make sure you succeed."

"Okay," said Geezer, "you're *sure* you haven't watched *Stellar Hike*?"

"Was that another quote?" Frexle said, looking sincerely interested.

"Not precisely," answered Geezer, "but you're using that same type of speak that they use."

"Interesting. I'll make it a point to watch a few episodes

while you're away. If you succeed, we'll have to talk about them; if not, well, then I guess we won't." There was no response to that. "So, are there any other questions?"

"Just one," said Harr. "How long do we have?"

"Ah, yes," Frexle said with an enthusiastic smile. "The Kallians are scheduled to start testing in two days."

"Swell," said Harr.

KALLIAN

*A*fter Frexle had left the *Reluctant*, the crew got busy with preparations. There wasn't a ton to do, but Harr wanted to make it look good since Vool was there. Fortunately, nobody questioned him in front of her. He deemed that simultaneously odd and pleasant.

Geezer had headed back down to his station and Harr pulled him up on the intercom.

"Coordinates plugged in, honcho."

Harr signaled Geezer to activate the switch and grinned as Vool held on to the console with a look of uncertainty.

A blink later, the *Reluctant* was hovering over Kallian. Geezer had set the cloak before activating the GONE drive, so Harr felt confident that they weren't seen. Still, he didn't like to leave things to chance so he got the crew checking over the planetary communications and also had them size up Kallian's level of sophistication. Vool had wanted them to just jump down to the planet and get things moving, but Harr decided it was better to know what they were getting into.

"Planet looks like it's nice enough from here," he said

while gazing at the floating marble that hung in the center of the main view.

"First time I've ever seen a planet of that color," said Sandoo.

"Greenish-pink is odd, I'll admit," Harr agreed. "Could mean that the air's not breathable."

"It shouldn't matter to any of us, sir."

"True, Commander, but it may matter to me."

"What do you mean, sir?"

"That I've grown somewhat fond of breathing oxygen," Harr said with his eyebrows raised.

"But, sir," Sandoo said in that motherly tone that came out whenever Harr was about to breach protocol, "you can't go down to that planet. It'd be against regulations."

"Whose regulations, Commander?"

"The Segnal Space Marine Corps, sir."

"Ah, yes, I see." Harr thought it best to go a little easy on Sandoo. The android was all about regulations, after all, and he was a damn good soldier. Arguably, he was the most by-the-book soldier that Harr had ever met. "In case you've forgotten, Commander, we're no longer a part of the SSMC."

Sandoo surveyed the area as if seeking a perch to stand on, and then said, "That's true, but we still have to adhere to some form of regulations or there will be anarchy."

Harr glanced away for a moment. Lieutenant Moon had three screens going full-time, each with either a stream of text or multiple video feeds pouring out. Ridly's layout wasn't much different except for the content she viewed was less fashion-based. Curr was wearing a set of what appeared to be headphones. That was peculiar, seeing that he could just plug straight into the console. There was likely something in his programming that preferred the old-fashioned route, or it could be that he was doing his best to dissuade Middleton from talking to him. Not that Middleton would have, since he was too busy working on the satellite data collection near the back of the bridge. Jezden, of course, was checking out the local porn.

"Commander," Harr said eventually, "I appreciate your concern. I honestly do. You're just doing your job and I respect that. Actually, I demand it. But please recall that we just had a conversation a few hours ago regarding why I'm in command of this ship. You were the one who made the observation that I'm the only person aboard this ship who thinks outside of the box."

"Except for Geezer," Sandoo answered with slump of his shoulders.

"Right, him too." Harr stood up and put his hand on Sandoo's shoulder. "My point is that I'm the most likely candidate for success here. If we succeed, we'll end up with more missions, and that means more times this is going to happen. There's no point in having this conversation every time. We're just going to have to change the way we think about some of our procedures. It's a new world, Commander. Time for us to make some new rules to go along with it."

In that moment, Sandoo seemed exceedingly human. His face was drawn and he even sighed in such a way that made his body appear distressed. "Yes, sir," he said in a ragged voice, "but I don't like it."

"I know you don't, and that's what makes you a solid commander."

Sandoo brightened a bit. "Thank you, sir."

By now, Jezden was over by Vool, making his first move. Harr had been surprised that he'd waited this long. She was too attractive for him not to take a shot. Plus, she was a "god," in a manner of speaking, which had to have the android's circuits buzzing.

"What's up, baby?" Jezden said in his smooth way.

"The ceiling?" answered Vool, looking upward.

Jezden let go a practiced laugh. "Good one. So, you new in town?"

"What town?"

"Look, babe," Jezden said, "I'm just trying to break the ice here, ya know?"

Vool furrowed her brow. "I see no ice."

"You're a pretty literal chick, huh? I like that in a woman. Of course, I can think of a number of things that I like in a woman. Me, for example."

"I sense you are trying to use a…pick-up line?"

"Got it in one," Jezden said with a wink.

"Got what in one?"

"I just meant…"

"Let's save some time," Vool said with smoldering eyes. "I'm an Overseer. You're a peasant, and not a very attractive one, at that."

"Excuse me?" Jezden's demeanor rapidly changed. "Not good looking? I'll have you know that I've bedded down more women in a weekend than most men do in their entire lives."

"I'm sure you're very impressed with that," noted Vool.

"Damn straight, I am. On top of that, I was voted the most likely to get laid at every adult convention I've ever been to, and I've been to many."

Vool blinked casually and said, "I can't imagine it's all that challenging to find a partner at an adult convention."

"And you're not exactly the hottest chick I've ever seen either, lady." Jezden was on fire now. "I was just trying to be nice to you. Throw you a bone. Literally."

"Well, soldier-boy," Vool said, tilting her head, "if you're done being nice, it would be great if you would return to your chair. Alternatively, I could just kill you, which I assure you would grant me a far better sensual response than anything you could muster sexually."

Jezden grimaced and shook his head at her. "You're one weird chick."

"You have no idea."

Harr felt a little respect for Vool from that, but he still didn't trust her. He'd had an operative along on his first mission with this crew who had turned out to be a complete lunatic. That man, too, was calm, cool, and collected when he talked about death and destruction. There was just something about the breed of natural-born killers that made Harr's skin crawl. He understood that being a soldier meant that he was going to be faced with fighting, and that often meant someone was going to end up on the wrong end of a laser beam, but unlike people such as Vool, Harr found no pleasure in the kill.

"Sir," Middleton said, having gotten back to his own desk during the exchange between Vool and Jezden, "I've found information regarding the person in charge of the warp research."

"Technically," argued Curr, "*I* found it, but go ahead and take the credit, Middleton. You always do."

"Cool, thanks," Middleton said with a fake grin. "Anyway, sir, the scientist's name is Dr. Rella DeKella and she works for a place called *Wagean Associated Research Program for Engineers and Designers*."

"The acronym is *W.A.R.P.E.D.*, sir," noted Curr.

"I got that, Ensign, thank you. Anything else, Middleton?"

"Just that she's done a few video statements on the upcoming test and it appears that they are on schedule."

Harr scratched his nose. "Anything you can put on-screen?"

"Sure."

The main view filled with the sight of a woman who was

roughly Harr's age. She had dishevelled brown hair, thick-rimmed dark glasses that slightly magnified her kaleidoscopic eyes, and she was clearly not all that competent in the field of wearing makeup.

"Slevb blurg glagger glinti-poot…"

"Sorry, sir," Middleton said, resetting the video. "I forgot to activate the Universal Translator."

"Idiot."

"Shut up, Curr."

"All of the components are in place for the test," Dr. DeKella said as she adjusted the collar of her white lab coat. Harr had already found her incredibly attractive, and the sound of her sultry, yet nerdy, voice only served to solidify his feelings. "We are running final evaluations and calculations to ensure that we've not missed anything. One can never be too careful when it comes to mathematical models. At this point, I see nothing that will derail a successful outcome."

"Beautiful," said Harr.

"What's that, sir?"

"Nothing, Commander," Harr said quickly. "Just find it, uh, beautiful when a project comes together."

"Ah," Sandoo said with a firm nod. "Couldn't agree more, sir."

"So she's the one you're going to kill?"

Harr did not allow himself to get irritated at this question. Instead, he calmly replied, "Only if necessary, Vool."

"Seems necessary to me."

"I'm sure it does, but seeing that Frexle left me in charge, it's really not your place to make any decisions in that regard. I'll make the call on who lives and who dies on this little adventure."

"Unless you fail," she reminded him, "which you most

likely will. Then it'll be up to me to make that call, and you can be certain that I won't hesitate."

"Until then, your role is to observe," Harr commanded.

"Continue talking to me like that, Harr, and I'll shove a shoe up your ass. And do believe me when I say that. I will quite literally do it. My shoe, your ass, full insertion."

Harr rolled his eyes and shook his head. She would not get the better of him. He'd already had experience working with that nutty operative in the past. Their kind had to have their little power-plays to make them feel superior. Harr was one who had been trained that the superior officer was to be respected. Not that he wouldn't counter orders if they seemed ridiculous, of course, but he'd always first try to find another way to accomplish a mission via an indirect route. People like Vool, though, they approached each mission the same way, through intimidation and violence, and the more of both the better.

"Ensign," Harr said to Middleton, "I noticed that Dr. DeKella has multicolored eyes. Is this normal to their species or is it particular to her?"

"All Kallians have that, sir. Also, they have tails."

"Sorry, did you say tails?"

"*I* was supposed to bring up the tails," Curr complained.

"You probably do, Curr," Middleton said with a laugh. "Besides, I can't help it that you're so slow."

"You're a jerk."

"You're a bonehead."

"Honestly," Harr interrupted the bickering before it got out of hand, "if you two don't get control of yourselves, I'm going to have to separate you." The two men glowered at each other momentarily before finally looking away. "Okay, so they have tails. Long tails? Short tails? What are we talking about here?"

Middleton grunted toward Curr. "Go ahead and tell him,

Curr. I wouldn't want to interfere with your incredibly important job."

"Jerk."

"Ass."

Harr cleared his throat, silencing them.

"Curr?" he said.

"Sorry, sir," Curr said tightly. "He's just…never mind. The tails are of all different lengths." Curr turned toward his console and put up a bunch of pictures of Kallians in all different angles. "If you look at their pants, sir, you'll see that they all have holes in the back, just under the belt line. That's where their tails hang out."

"It's odd that they have belt loopth at all," Moon said. "It's not like they need belts with those tails hanging out."

Harr found the outfits to be pretty much the same as Segnalian standard wear. Shoes, slacks, standard shirts, some button-up, some not, and a jacket. A few of the Kallians were even wearing ties. Then he saw a grouping of pictures that made him cock his head in contemplation.

"How come that one group of people has their pants hanging so low? Honestly, I can't even see how they can walk around like that."

"That's the younger crowd, sir," explained Curr. "It's the style to wear them like that."

"Looks like they have to hold them up with one hand," said Jezden. "Seems pointless."

"Ridiculous," agreed Harr.

"The older folks on Kallian would concur, sir," Curr said with a nod, "but, then again, they are old."

"Right."

"Thtyle is thtyle," Moon stated, shrugging.

This would mean a pretty radical alteration in their physical appearances. Multicolored contacts were easy enough for Geezer to manufacture, but tails would be tricky.

They'd also have to put together some clothing options that made sense. Nobody on his team was going to go with the low-hanging pants, though—of that he was certain.

"Lieutenant Moon," he said, "I'm putting you in charge of making us look the part."

"Sorry, thir," Moon said dubiously, "but are you selecting me for this job because I'm a man trapped in a woman's body?"

"No, Lieutenant, I'm selecting you because you're the most skilled person for the job."

"Oh." Moon sat up a little taller, smiling proudly. "Thank you, thir. Who will I be working on?"

Harr had put a lot of thought to that already. He wanted to have Sandoo along, but he was too much of a stickler for regulations. Moon was out of the question because Harr didn't know what the Kallian's societal norms were for Moon's particular situation. Harr was fine with it, but the Kallians might not be, and the last thing this team needed was to appear out of place. Middleton and Curr were too rambunctious when around each other. He could—and probably should—split them up, but he needed them here to help Sandoo monitor things. And, obviously, Geezer was always better off staying on the *Reluctant*.

"It'll be me, Ridly, and Jezden."

"And me," said Vool.

"Whoa, Captain," Jezden said while getting to his feet. "Nobody's putting a tail on me. I'll go for the eyes things 'cause that's pretty sweet, but a tail? I don't think so."

"I'm sorry, Jezden," Harr said with a hard stare, "did you mistake what I'd said for me *asking* if you wanted to go?"

"Huh? Well…"

"You're on this mission, like it or not, and that means you're getting a tail…like it or not."

Jezden was obviously fighting to keep his ire down. "Yes,

sir," he said through gritted teeth, "but I want to make sure it's as short as possible."

"Fine with me. I'll agree to whatever length Curr and Middleton find on the subject."

"I've been looking that up, sir," Middleton said. "It seems that leaders have longer tails, for some reason. Could just be coincidence."

"There ya go, Captain," Jezden said with a big stinking grin. "I can have a nice short tail and you can have one of those enormous boss ones. Comparing our backs will be just the opposite from comparing our fronts."

VOOL REPORTS

*V*ool moved to the quarters she was assigned and set up a connection with Veli. It wasn't the cleanest connection, but since he always hid from view anyway, it didn't really matter. She couldn't understand why he felt the need to hide who he was. Probably something to do with fear of assassination. Fact was, if she were hired to kill him, it wouldn't be that hard to find a flashlight.

"Vool," Veli said, "what have you learned?"

"Nothing much," she replied. "We just got here. The people on the planet have tails so I have to get one of those. Right now they're working on the crew, though. All in all, it's boring."

"I'm talking about what you've gleaned regarding the technology on that ship."

"Haven't checked," she said with a shrug.

"Well, will you?"

"I guess."

"You guess?" Veli sounded incensed, and that improved Vool's mood. She did so love irritating people. "Look, Vool, I know your father is a senator, but remember that I'm the

Lord Overseer. You can go about being as flippant as you wish with senators and the like, but it's not wise to be so with me."

"Or what, you'll kill me?" she said with a scoff. "Yawn. What do I care?"

"Okay," Veli said after a few moments, "let's try a different tact. Would you like to keep your ability to do your job?"

"If you're threatening to fire me, Veli, I'm not worried. There are plenty of people willing to hire me to exact my particular brand of work."

"Not if you're missing your limbs," Veli pointed out.

"I'm impressed," Vool said with a mischievous grin. "It takes a rare individual to find my leverage points."

"It takes a rare individual to ascend to the top of the Overseers," Veli responded. "Now, will you please find out what you can about that damn ship?"

"Fine," Vool said and then disconnected the call.

She could only hope that Veli was still speaking, thinking that she was still listening. He'd figure it out eventually.

ODD BEHAVIOR

*G*eezer had spent the last weeks poring over old records of how transporter systems could work. Nobody had a definitive answer as to the technology, and most scientists claimed it was a physical impossibility due to a number of factors. The *Meschoingberg Principle* spoke of the futility of determining position and momentum of quantum particles; the data storage necessary for even a single life would register in the tredecillion range; a beam with sufficient energy had not been identified, nor had one even come close; and the celebrated Segnalian Physicist, Dr. Lou Zaire, called the entire idea "a bag of hooey." On top of that, the *Clonographic Theory* stated you'd end up leaving a bunch of copies of yourself all over the place.

But things like that never stopped Geezer from working. In his estimation, the only reason that technology failed to advance was because people were not plugging the right stuff into the right place. It also didn't hurt that he never bored of trying different combinations of wiring, on everything from simple breadboards to complex matrix panels. Frankly, it could be argued that his tinkering thus far had given them many amazing pieces of tech already, including a few additional ones that he'd never bothered to report, such as his *Coffee-Tea Merge-O-Cuppa*, the *Triple-Headed Wratchett-Screwdriver*, and the *Multistudded Tonail Deatomizer*. All of which he planned to patent if the opportunity ever presented itself. He still wanted to market the *SSMC Reluctant* model that he'd created a long time back, as well. There just hadn't been time.

That thought made him wonder whatever happened to that little ship. He had created it as a test case to see if his instantaneous travel system worked. It had worked so well that a race of tiny people found the ship, took it over, and then tried to get back to the big ship so that they could thank them properly. The little fellow in charge, Liverbing, had been very helpful to the Platoon F crew during their last adventure, and it was the ship's engineer, a miniaturized replica of Geezer himself, who had unraveled cloaking technology. When they had parted, the other robot—named Goozer—was also working on a transporter. They had promised to share successes with each other, but since Geezer had heard nothing, he could only assume that nothing was found yet. Geezer had resolved to get in touch with Goozer at some point just to check on things, but there never seemed to be enough hours in the day. He couldn't help but wonder if the Overseers knew about that miniature crew, too, though.

He shrugged in his mechanical way and began putting together a new wiring configuration, but stopped because he noticed that Vool had entered the room. She seemed to be snooping around, which was odd since Geezer held no secrets.

"Something I can help you with?" he asked as diplomatically as he could manage.

"You could mind your own business, tin-man."

"Wow," Geezer said. "I haven't been called that in a while, but then I haven't been around a lot of classy ladies recently, either."

"Complimenting me isn't going to make me think more highly of you, metal-boy."

"Metal-boy? That's a new one." Geezer shook his head at her. "It's funny how you Overseers think you're so smart, so highly evolved, and yet here you are bandying about slurs like you're just a shade over ape." She didn't reply. "What the hell do you want in my engineering room, anyway?"

"I'm here to watch and judge," she answered as she continued searching for whatever it was she was searching for. "That means all parts of this ship and its crew. You just keep your mouth shut and do your job and I'll keep my report about you to a minimum."

"Ass," Geezer said.

"Everybody has one."

"I don't," Geezer pointed out, "unless you consider the company presently in this room."

"Impressive," said Vool with a huge, fake smile. "Did you think that up all by yourself, Mr. Steel?"

If it weren't for the fact that Vool was essentially a god and could deactivate him without much effort, and the additional fact that he was completely useless in the realm of fighting, he would have popped her one, square in the snoot.

"Just do what you've got to do and then get out, lady."

"I don't need your permission, you aluminum can."

"Unbelievable," Geezer said as he turned back to his work.

He'd suddenly thought of a few new places that he could stick some wires.

ABOUT TO DEPART

*E*veryone except Vool had their look in place. Seeing the world through all of the colors that made up his kaleidoscope contact lenses was definitely odd, but it was easily manageable when compared to carrying his infernal tail around. It took a solid 30 minutes of practice to quit knocking things off the shelves before Harr finally got the hang of it. Ridly picked it up immediately, of course, and Jezden's tail was so short that he didn't have to worry about a thing.

"You're sure this thing isn't going to fall off?" Ridly asked.

"If it does," answered Moon, "part of your bottom is going to come off with it. You've seen how the captain has been knocking his all over the place. If his stays on after all that wear and tear, I can't imagine why yours would be an issue." He turned toward Harr. "No offense, thir."

"None taken."

"At least Jezden got his wish," Ridly said, pointing at the tiny tail hanging off the back of the android.

"His wish was to not have one at all," Moon replied as he

walked over to check on Vool, who was in the heating chamber that each one of them had to endure before their tails could be affixed, "but Enthign Middleton found that the smallest recorded tail on Kallian was just under twelve inches in length. So I set Jezden's to precithely twelve inches."

"Should keep him balanced, anyway," Harr said under his breath.

"Thorry, thir?"

"Nothing. Nothing at all." Harr was now looking through the glass that separated his team from Vool. "So, did Geezer give you that tracking device for Vool's tail?"

"He did, thir." Moon picked up the tail, keeping it just under the lip of the window, and showed him where the miniature device was embedded. Vool would be none the wiser. "As soon as she's warmed up enough, I'll attach it and she'll be traceable. Geezer also put the cameras in her contact lenses. They are incredibly thin and cover the entire surface of the lens, so she'll never even know that we can see what she's doing."

"Perfect." Harr turned to Sandoo, who had been standing there the entire time with his trademark look of anxiety. "I'm counting on you and Geezer to keep tabs on her every move, Commander. I don't trust her. She's too flippant about death and killing."

"Like Yek, sir," Sandoo said, referring to the crazy operative who had been on their first mission.

"Exactly."

"Nice tail, Captain," Jezden said as he walked into the room.

"Marks me as the leader, Ensign."

"Marks you as a dork," Jezden said with a laugh. "Looks ridiculous."

"To us, yes," Harr retorted, even though he couldn't help

but agree, "but to the people we're visiting, it would be more ridiculous if we didn't have them at all."

"Well, I'm glad that mine is as small as it is." A grin came over his face. "Now *that's* something I'd never thought I'd say."

The heating chamber dinged to let everyone know that Vool's body temperature had climbed to the required level for Moon to attach the tail. The lieutenant shooed everyone out of the room so that he could get to work. This gave Harr the perfect alibi to visit engineering.

Getting there wasn't much fun since climbing down a ladder with the big, whopping tail hanging off his backside was quite a chore. It made him wonder how he was going to manage dealing with other things, such as bodily issues. One more reason that being an android would have had its advantages.

"Hey, Geezer," Harr said as he carefully walked into the room.

"Nice tail, honcho."

"Any update on the map for Kallian?"

"Curr's taken care of getting that data, but I've been working on hooking everything into your contact lens. Trickier than I'd expected. By the time you land, I'll have completed uploading all of their schematics to it. Don't have time to section it out."

"Is that a bad thing?" asked Harr.

"Just means that wherever you are, you'll see an overlay in the upper-right of your vision describing pretty much anything you're looking at."

"In addition to the maps, you mean?"

"Yep."

"What kind of things are we talking here, Geezer?"

"Well, you'll see stuff like the ingredients of a plate of food, for example."

"Couldn't I just see that by looking at the plate?"

"Deeper than that, honcho. I'm talking about it detailing the fat, sugars, and all that stuff."

Harr stood back, admiring his engineer's craftiness. "Actually, that sounds like a pretty damned useful tool."

"Yeah?" Geezer's eyes glowed for a second.

"Anyway," Harr said before Geezer could go off on one of his marketing tangents, "as I was telling Sandoo, I want you both to keep an eye on everything Vool does."

"Already planning on it, big cat. Don't trust that one at all. She's a complete assh…"

"I know how you feel about her, Geezer," Harr interrupted. "Sadly, I share in that sentiment, which is why I want her under constant surveillance."

"Consider it done, chief. If she so much as shits sideways, you'll be the first to know."

"Actually," Harr said with a look of disgust, "I think I'll pass on knowing that much."

"Oh? Okay, one sec, then." He typed something on his screen. "Done. We'll leave out bathroom habits in our report. I sometimes forget how squeamish you humans get about things like that."

"Wait, you were seriously planning to tell me about…" He paused, closed his eyes for a moment, and then shook his head. "Never mind. Were you able to get the identification badges?"

"Sure did." The robot turned and grabbed a tray that contained a small stack of IDs. "Got the perfect M.O. for you, too."

"Oh?"

"Well, Middleton gets the credit, really," Geezer said while fishing through the badges. Chances are that Curr was the one to really get the credit if Middleton was claiming it. "He did a little research and found out that there's a group of inspectors slated to arrive at the W.A.R.P.E.D. building this afternoon. Once I got the full details, I intercepted their transport unit—something called an 'arrow plane'—and had it grounded on a deserted island. I also cut off all their communications. They'll have no way to tell anyone what's happened, so you'll be able to take their places with ease."

Harr thought about this for a moment. "Won't there be someone waiting for them on the other side?"

"According to all the records we've found, nobody even knows what they look like. Apparently, they keep all inspectors under a strict rule of anonymity so that they can't be bribed or threatened. Helps ensure non-biased testing and verification. According to the documents, they even undergo plastic surgery to change their appearance at the end of each inspection."

"That's awfully convenient," said Harr.

"It surely is," Geezer said with the equivalent of a robotic cough. "They can only do a set number of projects, too, or they'll end up with skin so tight that they look like they're permanently smiling."

"Well, that's creepy."

"Yeah. Anyway, my plan is that you'll each be assigned the identity of their inspectors. You'll get their names and credentials, just in case someone does a call-in verification or something."

"I thought these people were kept anonymous?"

"Not from the sleuthing skills on this ship, prime. Our tech is a fair bit more advanced than theirs."

"Brilliant."

"Only way I know, big cat."

"One last question," Harr asked before leaving the room, "did you locate that tracking device that Frexle put on the ship?"

"Can't find it anywhere, chief."

"Well, keep an eye out, will you?"

"No can do, honcho," Geezer said dryly. "I need them both in if I'm going to be productive."

Harr looked at his engineer and sighed. "Everyone's a comedian."

THE ARRIVAL

*I*t used to be dicey flying a shuttle down to a planet's surface, but ever since Geezer had hooked up the cloaking technology that Goozer had shared with him, landings were as stealthy as slipping past a sleeping sloth.

They'd landed just outside of the city in a manmade recreational area that the map named "Central Hangout." At first, Harr was concerned by this name because it implied that it would be overrun with people. Life scans showed the opposite. There were very few people in the area. This could have had something to do with local time being morning, which Harr assumed meant that everyone was on their way to work.

"Everyone has their translators connected?" he asked as he verified his own was working. They all nodded in response. "Good. Now, we all know the drill here."

"I don't," said Vool.

"True. Okay, it's simple. Don't act like…well, you. Pretend you're normal."

Vool crossed her arms and undoubtedly began thinking

up many clever ways to end Harr's life. He didn't care. Fact was that completing this mission was a long shot, so she'd probably get her wish anyway. But until that fateful moment, he was going to keep being the captain of this crew, and that meant that Vool had to be in a constant state of questioning things.

Ridly finished up her ship check, setting it to return to the *Reluctant* once they had departed. "Scans in the immediate area show no signs of life," she said as Harr watched over her shoulder. "Shuttle is clear. We can hop out and he'll fly back to the *Reluctant*."

"I'm sorry," said Jezden, "did you just refer to the shuttle as a *he?*"

"What's wrong with that?" asked Ridly. "You all refer to the *Reluctant* as *she*, so why can't I call this one a *he?*"

"Because everyone knows that ships are female, that's why," Jezden answered. "The captain is a man so the ship is a woman. Just how it works."

"You're walking on eggshells, Jezden," Harr warned him.

"Why?"

"Because you're an idiot," Ridly said. "Not all captains are men, you know? And who's to say that Captain Harr isn't gay?"

"Uh, me?" Harr replied incredulously.

"Was just making a point, Captain," Ridly said apologetically. "I didn't mean to out you like this."

"No, I am *not* gay," Harr said more anxiously than he should have. "Not that there's anything wrong with being gay. I mean, I have gay friends."

"They're called boyfriends," Vool said.

"Not like that," said Harr. "Forget it."

"Sorry, sir," said Ridly.

Jezden gave Harr the once over. "Come to think of it, she's right."

"Wait a second here…"

"No, really, you did serve under Rear Admiral Parfait," Jezden said and then giggled at his own sentence.

"He was my boss!"

"Those meetings tended to run a little long," Jezden mused.

"It does look suspicious, sir," Ridly stated with a shrug.

"Yeah, okay," Jezden said, "so the *Reluctant's* a he, too, then."

Harr just stood there, blinking at them both.

Vool seemed to be enjoying the entire exchange. If nothing else, she'd cracked a smile for the first time since they'd met. You would think that her smile would have taken her already-amazing looks and pleasurably intensified them. It didn't. She had the smile of a hungry wolf.

"I'm going to use the can while you idiots get things ready," Vool said.

"Let me just state for the record that I am *not* gay," Harr said stiffly the moment that Vool closed the lavatory door.

"You said that pretty stiffly," Jezden noted. "It's nothing to be ashamed of, Captain. Explains a lot, too."

"If I were gay, I wouldn't be ashamed of it, but I'm…" Harr stopped replaying Jezden's last sentence in his mind. "Explains what, exactly?"

"Well, your lack of bedding down with any women, for one."

"You may recall, Ensign, that I'm the only human on the *Reluctant*."

"So?"

"Well, who am I supposed to have relations with?" Harr asked incredulously.

"Ridly?" suggested Jezden.

"No, thank you," Ridly stated a little too quickly. "No

offense, Captain. You're an all-right-looking guy and all, but I don't do gay guys."

"I'm not gay!"

"There's always Lieutenant Moon," Jezden said. "Best of both worlds, sort of. I mean, I'm only into chicks, but with the recent light being shed on your particular interests…"

"Okay, that's enough," Harr commanded as he walked to the back hatch. "You two can think what you want about me. I honestly don't care. Let's just get to business and quit the chatter."

"Quick to anger," Ridly said sideways.

"I'm telling ya," Jezden agreed as Harr reached for the container that held their badges, "things are all starting to fall into place now."

Harr grabbed the container and forced himself calm. What did he care what they thought about his sexuality? The fact was that he had sorely missed the touch of a woman. Unfortunately, no matter how he might try, he could never see an android as anything more than a sophisticated computer. At least not in the way of intimacy. Yes, they were all *very* human in their own ways; and it was true that even the homeliest among them (Curr) was still better looking than most actual humans; and it was also true that if Lieutenant Moon had instead decided to become one of the female personalities who originally shared his mental space, Harr would have likely tried to build a relationship with *her*. But Moon hadn't, and so that was that. Ridly, good looking or not, was simply not his type.

Vool stepped out of the restroom as Harr pushed the current conversation out of his mind and set to focus on the task at hand.

"Listen up," he said in a voice that conveyed the "gay talk" was over, "Geezer was able to get us identification cards and credentials. We're going to play the part of systems inspectors on this warp test. Our job, as far as the Kallians are concerned, is to make sure everything about the test is safe." He glanced over at Vool. "Obviously, our actual goal is to sabotage things, but only on my orders. Is everyone clear?"

"Yeah, whatever," Vool said as the other two nodded.

"Good. Now, let me hand these out." He pulled out the first badge and handed it to Ridly. "You're going to be Dr. Fleeka Baloo."

"Ooh," Ridly said with a big grin, "I like that name."

"Swell," said Harr as he handed out the next badge. "Vool, you're going to be Dr. Grayle Piffer."

"Yay."

Harr studied the two remaining cards, checking the titles on both. "Since I'm in charge of this little mission, I'll have to be a Dr. Zep Welder." He fastened the badge to his white lab coat and then glanced down at the last of the badges. "That means, Jezden, that you're going to be Dr. Dangly N. Impotent."

"Dangly N. Impotent?" Jezden said, snatching the ID away from Harr. "What? That sounds awful. I can't be that!"

"Sorry, Jezden," said Harr, not feeling the least bit sorry, "but that's all that's left."

"But this is a horrible name. I mean, even *I* feel bad for the poor sucker who actually has to suffer with this name."

Harr fought to withhold his grin. "I'm sure it doesn't mean the same thing to the Kallians as it does to us. Remember that we are using Universal Translators. For all we know, when they hear that name it could be like us hearing 'Jack Preston' or something else innocuous."

"I hope so," Jezden said, irritably fastening the badge to his coat. "Horrendous."

OLD HORK CITY

They stepped off the transport and started walking due north. Harr's heads-up map took some getting used to as he led the team through the trees toward the city. Every tree he saw flooded the upper-right of his vision with details about its composition. Age, bark density, sap consistency, if any, and even levels of infestation scrolled in a never-ending stream of information. After walking for a while like this, he was finally able to ignore the influx of data and focus instead on the map.

Behind them, the dampened sound of engines signaled that the shuttle was returning to the *Reluctant*. If nothing else, that made Harr happy. The last thing he needed was for some jogger to run through the woods and smack into the side of an unseen ship.

They cleared the trees and found a city that was bustling with activity. Vehicles were zipping this way and that on the main road and pedestrians were crowding the sidewalks. The sound was almost deafening, especially when the larger vehicles sped on by.

"That's a lot of buildings," Ridly said.

"You should see what I see," Harr replied, referring to the map in his display. "We have to cross this street and head a couple of blocks down. We're looking for something called the underground. Apparently, there is a monorail-type system that will take us deeper into the city."

Getting across the street was similar to how it was done on Segnal. They waited at one of the corners until a traffic light changed, and then they walked across while dodging the vehicles that cared little about the status of traffic lights.

"That was fun," Jezden said after smacking the back of one of the vehicles, which resulted in the driver honking a horn and putting up his pinky. Harr assumed that was the Kallian equivalent to the Segnalian thumb.

"Stop for a second," he said. "I need to get my bearings."

He took a step forward and nearly knocked over a passerby.

"Watch where you're going, moron," the guy said while checking over his clothes.

"Sorry," Harr replied. "We're new in town and…"

"I think you've mistaken me for someone who gives a crap," said the man.

"Want me to kill him?" asked Vool.

The man scurried away under the gaze of the Overseer.

"Vool," Harr warned, "I don't think it's wise to mention your desire to kill anyone. You're bound to get us all arrested."

"If they arrest me," she said, "I'll just kill them, too."

"How about you just stop talking about killing people?"

"You're not the boss of me," she retorted.

"Actually, for this mission, I am."

She growled. "Fine."

"Thank you."

"Excuse me," a young woman said to Harr. She was

dressed sharply, had neatly cropped hair, and was carrying an attaché case.

"Yes?" said Harr.

"I was wondering if you four happened to own this piece of the sidewalk?"

Harr frowned for a moment. "No," he said slowly.

"Are you sure?" she said with a squint. "Maybe you have a deed somewhere on your person?"

"I don't think so."

"That's strange, then. You see, I ask because you're standing directly in the way as everyone is trying to get to work, and that can only mean that you either own this piece of concrete or you're a complete prick."

"Oh," Harr said, putting his hands up. "I'm sorry, we're just new to the area and a bit lost…"

"Well, get lost in a corner, buddy," she said menacingly and then pushed on by, holding up her pinky.

Vool showed her smile for the second time that day.

"Sure are a hostile people," noted Ridly.

"Straight shooters, if you ask me," said Jezden as he stepped out and watched the Kallian that had just chastised Harr as she headed down the sidewalk. "I kind of like it."

"Hey, short-tail," said a grumbly looking man who was blocked by Jezden, "how about moving outta the way so someone with a bit of length can get to work on time, eh?"

Jezden stepped aside. His mouth was hanging open. "Did he just call me short-tail?"

"If the tail fits," Ridly said with a grin. "Still glad they speak their minds, hotshot?"

"Ridly, not now," Harr said. "Let's keep moving."

From Harr's perspective, walking with a purpose seemed to keep everyone in line. People still grunted at him if they had to step around, but they didn't stop to speak their minds. It was just like his father had once told him when he was growing up, "If you keep your eyes ahead," he'd said, "and act like you know where you're going, people will often get out of your way." So far that had proved true. What was most baffling to Harr was how these people could live like this. Even the busiest times in Segnal's capital city weren't this bad.

As they continued walking toward the underground, he couldn't help but feel his stomach growl at the smell of the foods that were being sold from carts littering the sides of the road. The owners were calling out to pedestrians, offering samples and deals. That, of course, made Harr wonder about currency. Obviously, they had nothing, and he'd forgotten to ask Geezer to hook them up.

Following a group of others, Harr led the crew down a flight of stairs and into an underworld labyrinth that was full of shops and kiosks. There was also a large train that was in the process of dumping off one set of passengers as another set struggled to hop on.

Trying to keep up with the crowd, they walked to the entryway and found that it was blocked by a metal bar. Harr took a glimpse to his left and saw people putting slips of papers into the machine that was attached to the bar. Once they slid it in, the bar would lift up and let them through, only to close again to stop the next person.

"Come on, pal," a guy standing behind them said, "let's move it, yeah?"

"Push back, Jezden," Harr said. "We need to get some papers or something."

The people around them were making nasty comments as they finally got out of the way. All in all, it made Harr wonder if Vool might have the right of it. To be fair, though, Harr understood. These were just a bunch of people who were all likely grumpy about having to go into jobs that they didn't much enjoy.

"Over there, sir," Ridly said, pointing at a station that had a sign that read, "TICKETS."

It took some doing, but they muscled through the crowd and got to the counter.

"Yeah?" said the lady behind the glass. She gave the impression of being even grumpier than the woman who had given Harr the pinky.

"We need tickets, please."

"To where?"

"The, uh, W.A.R.P.E.D. building."

"I don't know every building in this town, mister," the lady said with a grunt. "What part of the city?"

Harr scanned through the map in his visual unit until he spotted the building. Then he zoomed out until he finally saw a word that appeared to describe the general area.

"Downtown?" he said, hopefully.

"Five credits," the lady said. "Each."

"Right," Harr said, patting his pockets for no apparent reason. "Five credits, you say?"

"Each."

"Just a moment, please," he said. He then pulled the others around to the side of the booth. "I don't suppose anyone has any credits?" They all just eyeballed him. "Right. Well, somehow we need to get twenty of them. Ideas?"

"We could kill someone and take what we need," suggested Vool.

"I'd rather not," Harr replied with a frown.

"Wuss."

"We could just walk," Ridly said. "It's not that far."

"For you, maybe." Harr glanced back up the stairs that they'd come down earlier. "Frankly, I'd rather not go back up into that mess of people."

"I agree," Jezden said. "No thanks. I'll just ask some lady and we'll have the money." He stepped out toward one particularly attractive Kallian. "Pardon me, miss," said Jezden with his winning smile, "we're trying to get downtown and we're short twenty credits. Could you help us?"

"Get a job, tiny-tail," the lady said, pushing Jezden out of her way.

Harr nearly snorted as Ridly let out an all-out laugh. Even Vool giggled slightly, which sounded incredibly like an angry chipmunk.

"What's with all the name calling about my tail?" Jezden asked, looking very hurt indeed.

"I don't know," Harr said, "but it gives me an idea." He stepped up to the next lady that passed by. "Excuse me, but could you spare twenty credits? I forgot my wallet at home and we need to get downtown."

The lady started to give him a once over. On a whim, he turned and showed her his tail. This made him feel very exposed, but the look on her face said that it was the right thing to do.

"Here you go, sugar," she said, slipping double the amount into his hand. "Also, take my card. Give me a call sometime and I'll gladly think up any number of ways that you can pay me back."

"Great," Harr said, wondering if he should be feeling as dirty as he did. "Thank you very much."

"Call me," she said with a wink before walking toward the turnstiles.

"No way," Jezden said. "That did *not* just happen."

"Forty credits say it did, Ensign," Harr replied while waving the bills in the android's face.

"Good call on wanting that short tail, Jezden."

"Shut up, Ridly," Jezden said, and then added, "Damn it."

THE TRAM

Getting on the tram was just about as much fun as buying the tickets. People were pushing and pulling and slamming into each other. Harr felt like a rag doll that was being fought over by triplets.

Vool tapped him on the shoulder and tilted her head toward the last car. There was hardly any foot traffic down there. The crew quickly walked over and stepped inside. It was nearly empty, aside from the group of kids that were laughing, yelling, and blaring some form of distorted music. Harr could deal with that, though. It wasn't like it was going to be a long trip.

They sat in the very back and Harr leaned in so they could hear him. "When we get there, you'll have to let me do all the talking. We need these people to think that I'm the bigwig on the team and that you're all my assistants."

"Yes, sir," Ridly said.

"Whatever," said Vool as she leaned back and crossed her arms.

Jezden hadn't seemed to have been paying much attention. "I should have gone with the bigger tail," he said tiredly. "Still," he peered up at Harr, "I'm good looking, right? I mean, I'm *definitely* better looking than you, yeah?"

"Stow it, Ensign," Harr replied with a frown. "Keep your mind on the mission."

"Easy for you to say."

The music stopped abruptly. Harr glanced up to see a couple of young Kallians staring at him. Their stares were somewhat menacing, which didn't seem much different than what he'd gotten from most of the Kallians he'd run into this morning.

One of the teens, a lanky fellow with stringy hair and a particularly insistent scowl, walked through the car, directly toward them. Behind him was a taller, bulkier teenager who seemed more dubious than irritable.

"Well, well, well," said the scowler in a leathery voice, "what do we have here? Looks like we have some oldies sitting in our chairs. Don't it, Yezto?"

"That it does, Weez," said Yezto. "That it does."

"What happens to people who sit in our section, Yezto?"

"They get roughed-up, Weez."

"Shame, that," Weez said, looking as though he didn't consider it to be shameful in the least. "Rules is rules, though, so who wants to go first?"

"Why don't you guys just move along?" Harr suggested. "We don't want any trouble."

"Oh," Weez answered with a nod. "They don't want any trouble, Yezto. We should probably just move along."

"Right. Let's just forget all about this happening, eh, Weez?"

Weez leaned in toward Harr, who sat back and prepared himself for a fight. "Maybe you're just a tough guy, old man. That what it is?" Harr said nothing. "I think that's what he thinks, Yezto. What do you think?"

"Sounds like it, Weez."

Vool uncrossed her arms and focused imploringly on Harr. "I could…" She paused and shrugged. "Well, you know."

"I do know," Harr said, "and I thank you for not saying it. But, I don't think it will be necessary."

Weez stood back up. "What are you two talking about?"

"Nothing for you to worry about," Harr said tightly. "Look, we're sorry we're in your seats. We're new to town and didn't know about any particular seating arrangements."

"Doesn't matter where you're sitting on this tram, gramps," said Weez. "They're all our seats."

So that's how it was, was it? These were the same types of little boneheads that Harr had dealt with when growing up. It was one of the reasons he'd joined the SSMC in the first place. He wanted to learn how to fight to defend himself. More than that, he wanted to defend others against the likes of bullies like these punks. But he had to keep his cool. He was leading this party and he didn't need the team's cover blown due to an argument on a transportation vessel.

Unfortunately, Jezden didn't seem to see it that way. "Listen, you little turd," the android said with a sneer that matched the one Weez wore, "why don't you walk away before I punch you in the neck?"

"Ensign…uh, I mean, Dr. Impotent," Harr said with a shake of his head, "that's uncalled for."

"Oooh," Weez said with a mock laugh. "Looks like we got us a real tough guy here, Yezto. And a doctor, at that. Well, Dr. Tough-guy…"

"Better than Dr. Impotent," Jezden muttered.

"…things are about to get very real."

Weez took a quick step forward, his fist raised and ready to strike, when Lieutenant Ridly reacted. The speed at which an android could move was that of the blink of an eye. She jumped up, stepped between Weez and Jezden, and landed a knee in the poor kid's groin with such ferocity that Harr thought certain that the kid's balls were going to fly out of his ass. Weez screeched and dropped to the floor as Ridly placed her foot on his neck.

Yezto jumped to the aid of his fallen friend, but Vool moved even faster than Ridly as she snaked a punch to the side of the boy's shoulder. He quite literally flew through the air and slammed into the side wall of the tram. Harr could only blink at the realization that Vool had just proved how powerful Overseers were. He'd known that they had the technology, but her speed and power was unfathomable. Thank goodness she hadn't knocked the kid in the head because it would have exploded.

Harr leaned down to Weez's face as Yezto squirmed in agony a few feet away.

"I really wish you would have just moved along," said Harr sadly. "This all could have been avoided."

Weez grunted a few times until Harr signaled Ridly to remove her foot from the kid's neck. Then Weez, looking like a mouse that was cornered by a group of hungry cats, said in a voice that was much higher-pitched than it had been pre-Ridly, "You're not supposed to hit us. We're under age."

"Again," Harr said as a slurry of expletives rang out in his head, "we're new to the area and didn't know that." He then leaned in a little closer and whispered, "Look, kid, I'll make a deal with you. You see that woman over there?" He motioned toward Vool, but Weez looked up at Ridly. "No, not the one that knocked your nuts into next week. I'm talking about the one that punched your pal in the shoulder and sent him flying." Weez nodded, still grimacing. "If you get up and act like none of this happened, and if you never...and I *do* mean *never*...tell anyone about any of this, I'll make sure that she doesn't hunt you down and kill you." Weez's eyes grew to the point of popping out. "Trust me on this, kid, she'll do just that. She kind of enjoys doing it."

"What the hell kind of doctors are you?" Weez asked with a frightened gasp.

"Depends on you, Weez," Harr said casually. "Normally, we're just inspectors, but we could easily find our way into the field of proctology, if you see where I'm going." Weez swallowed hard. "Now, do we have a deal, son?"

"Deal," said Weez as he struggled to get up. He continued clutching his groin while shuffling back to the other side of the car. Yezto was right on his tail and the remaining kids were all consciously avoiding eye contact.

"I thought you said I wasn't allowed to kill anyone?" Vool said.

"And you didn't," Harr noted.

"Right, but if they tell anyone, I can? That's what you told him."

"I don't think it will come to that, Vool," Harr replied. "You saw how scared that kid was."

"Yes," she said in an almost sultry voice that made Harr's skin crawl. "I sure hope one of them tells."

"Even if they do, you're not killing anyone."

Vool sighed and then fell back into her chair with a reaction that mimicked the age level of Weez and his friends. "All this 'not-killing people' is tiresome."

If it wasn't solidified before, it sure as hell was now. There was no way Harr was going to trust this particular Overseer. Frankly, it was unlikely that he'd ever trust any of them.

THE W.A.R.P.E.D. BUILDING

*T*he tram pulled out of the underground and came to a stop at street level, allowing the crew to avoid walking through another subterranean obstacle course.

Harr's visual map showed that the W.A.R.P.E.D. building was the one with the reflective, green glass windows that sat directly ahead. Where the streets near the landing site were a bustle of activity, these streets were doubly so. Taking a different tact than before, he began walking just as purposefully through the crowd as everyone else did.

They got to the building with little fuss and pushed through the main doors like they owned the place. He walked past the guard desk with a quick wave to the man who was holding the post.

"Excuse me, sir," the guard called out as Harr walked on by, "I need to see your badge."

"Hmmm?"

"Your badge, please?"

"Oh, right," Harr said, holding up the badge that Geezer had fastened for him. "The name is Dr., uh…"—he checked his badge— "...Zep Welder. My crew and I are here to do the final inspection on the warp technology before the big test."

"The inspection team?" the guard said, sitting up straight. Obviously inspection teams pulled some weight on this planet. "Oh, well, I'll contact Dr. DeKella straightaway. If you would please take a seat in the lobby over there, sir, I'll have her down here to meet you as quickly as possible."

Harr nodded before heading over to the plush leather chairs that sat off the main entrance. It was behind a glass enclosure that gave the crew a bit of privacy. Of course, it could have been bugged. He was going to check the armband that Geezer had made him a few weeks earlier, but he wasn't sure how. It had all sorts of gadgets built in, one of which was supposedly a surveillance detector. He studied it for a few moments before turning to Ridly.

"Any listening devices in here?"

She paused for a moment and then shook her head. "It's clear."

"Okay," he said to the team, "remember to let me do the talking."

"You won't be able to fool them," Vool said with her disbelieving duck-faced look. "This would all be far simpler if we just..."

"Kill them?" Harr finished, looking at her in disbelief. "Yeah, I know. You've made your position clear. Saying it over and over again is not going to change my mind. We're not killing anyone. Get that through your head already."

"Unless we have to," Vool said, not even looking slightly peeved.

"They're not even paying attention to me," said Jezden out of the blue. "It's like I don't even exist."

Ridly groaned and rolled her eyes. "You're worse than Vool, Jezden."

"His name is Dr. Impotent, Ridly," Harr said. "We have to stay in character here. No slip-ups."

"You just called me Ridly," she replied with a smirk. "It's Dr. Baloo."

"Damn," Harr said. "This is going to be a challenge."

Jezden sighed. "This is going to be a nightmare."

Harr saw movement out near the guard. There she was, the woman who had been displayed on the *Reluctant's* main screen talking about the warp technology. She was just as stunning in person. He rose to his feet as she walked into the room and reached her hand out in greeting.

"Hello," she said nervously. "I'm Dr. Rella DeKella. Well, I mean, I'm sure you already knew that. You *are* the inspectors, right?" She let out an awkward laugh. Was she sweating? "I'm rambling already. I do that when I'm nervous." Her face registered shock. "Not that I'm nervous. I don't want you to think that I'm nervous. Even though I just told you that I ramble when I'm nervous, and I'm clearly rambling." She stopped for a moment, spun away from them and whispered to herself just loudly enough for Harr to hear. "Get yourself together, Rella. This is the big time. Make it happen. *Make it happen.*" She took a deep breath, squared her shoulders, and turned back to Harr. "Let's try that again, shall we?" Her voice was slightly calmer now. "As I said, I'm Dr. DeKella. May I ask who is in charge here?"

"Uh," Harr said, feeling confused, "I thought you were."

She laughed again and then caught herself. "Sorry. I mean who is in charge of your group?"

"Oh, that would be me," Harr replied, "Captain Don Harr."

"Sir?" Ridly said, knocking him in the arm.

"Idiot," Vool announced with a smirk.

"Sorry," DeKella said. "What was that again?"

Harr wanted to punch himself. "Uh, sorry, was just trying to lighten the mood with a joke. Obviously, it failed."

"Oh, a joke? Haha! That's great. Most inspectors are so uptight." She appeared worried again. "Which is completely understandable. I mean, the work you do is very important. I wouldn't want you to think…"

"It's okay," he said, trying to calm her before she began to hyperventilate. "My name is Dr. Zep Welder."

"Nice to meet you, Dr. Welder," she said while gathering herself together again.

Harr motioned toward Vool. "This is Dr. Grayle Piffer."

"If you have made any mistakes," Vool said, stepping forward, "we will find them."

"Haha! You guys are great!"

"Actually," Harr said, "she was being serious. Dr. Piffer has no sense of humor."

"Oh," DeKella said after a moment. "My apologies, Dr. Piffer. I thought—"

"No harm done," Harr interrupted before she started to ramble again, even though he had to admit that he found that personality quirk just as attractive as the rest of her. "These are my other associates," Harr said with a quick wave toward Ridly and Jezden, "Dr. Fleeka Baloo and Dr. Dangly N. Impotent."

DeKella stepped over to Ridly and put out her hand. "Nice to meet you, Dr. Impotent."

"No," Ridly said, "I'm Dr. Baloo."

"Ah, right."

Jezden pushed himself to his feet. "I'm Impotent."

"That's too bad," DeKella said with a look of sympathy. "I understand that there are plenty of medicines on the market that can help with that these days, you know. It's nothing you have to live with."

"See?" Jezden said, turning to Harr for a moment. "I told you it meant the same…" He grunted and bit his lip for a moment. "My *name* is Dr. Impotent. My sexual status is just fine, thank you very much."

"Oh! I'm sorry. I'm just off my game at the moment. I meant no offense. There's just so much going on with trying to get all the last-minute preparations squared away. Plus," she said, "you have that incredibly tiny tail, so I just assumed…" She blanched again. "I'm sorry. I'm rambling again."

"It's okay," Harr said with a genuine smile. "You can relax. We're only here to make sure that things go the way they should. We're not your enemy."

"Really?" DeKella replied with a look of relief. "You mean that?"

"I do."

"Thank goodness. The last set of inspectors that came through here tried to blow everything up. It was terrible."

"Blow everything up?"

"Oh, you know what I mean," she said. "They were taking every little problem and making it seem catastrophic."

"Ah, yes," said Harr with a nod. "Well, you know Quality Assurance people. There's no gray with them…erm, us. We see things in black and white. Misspelling a word to us is just as bad as forgetting to connect a wire that will result in the destruction of a small city."

"Exactly!"

"That's why we were selected for our jobs, Dr. DeKella. If we are lax about things, what would be the point of assuring quality at all?"

"I suppose that makes sense," she answered thoughtfully. "I'd never really considered your side of things before."

"We get that a lot," Harr said, remembering his first job in the Segnal Space Marine Corps. He was in charge of finding every single issue with a new computer component that the

SSMC was using on remote detonators. He'd spent days poring over tests, documenting things to the tiniest detail, only to hand it in to his commanding officer to watch it get dropped in the trash. The officer then commanded that Harr write up a new report saying that everything was perfect. He had tried to argue, but after being threatened with a month of KP duty, he cleared the project. Two weeks later, eleven of the damn devices went off without provocation, causing damage to three ships and a large chunk of space rail. Harr ended up being blamed, costing him six months of KP duty. "Our job *is* to find issues," he continued, "but many QA folks get snippy because the reports we slave over are often ignored. That's why we tend to take things somewhat personally. The fact is that all we want is to ensure a product to be safe and free of issues."

"Huh," DeKella said with a tilt of her head, "I never really considered your group's feelings, Dr. Welder."

"Few do," he replied as Dr. DeKella began twisting her hair around her finger. "So," Harr said quickly, "where do we start?"

"Yes, right." DeKella dropped her hand. "Just follow me and I'll give you all a tour of our fine facility."

THE MCCARTHY SNIP-N-TAPE

*D*r. DeKella took them back outside. At first this seemed odd to Harr, but when she showed them the antenna arrays, the satellite dishes, the power grid connections, and the sludge runoff collectors, it all made sense. They were *supposed* to be inspectors, after all.

"Now we'll just need to get your badges updated here at the front desk," she said as they approached the guard who had stopped them earlier. "Mr. Ollap," she said to the uniformed man, "could you please give them full access to the facility?"

"Yes, ma'am," he replied as they handed over their badges. He typed away at a terminal and swiped the cards a few times, but there appeared to be a problem. "For some reason, I can't get these badges to connect. That's really strange. They're supposed to be universal."

Harr licked his lips. "Ah, yes," he said, "those are from the new Inspector's Line. We just got them last week. My boss said that there would probably be issues with those due to required software upgrades. You'd have thought that our group would QA our own badges, but production schedules ruled that possibility out. Typical. Anyway, you'll probably have the new updates within a week or so." By then, thought Harr, Platoon F would either be gone or the entire planet of Kallian would be.

"Got it," the guard replied. "Happens to us all the time. A cutting-edge facility like this should be on the cusp of this sort of technology, but we're always a couple of weeks behind." He fished around the desk for a moment and pulled out a couple of black, thumb-sized objects, typed a few more times on the computer, and started handing them out. "Okay, these fobs will give you full access to the facility, 32/9."

"32/9?" said Ridly.

"Thirty-two hours a day, nine days a week," the guard said with a squint.

"Oh, right, of course," Ridly said, shaking her head. "I'm already in mathematical mode. Thought you were using division...never mind."

The guard smiled. "The only places you won't have access to are the upper-levels where the executives and military personnel are stationed."

"Military?" said Harr, looking at DeKella.

"It's where the majority of our funding comes from, Dr. Welder," she said, after she thanked the guard and began leading them toward a set of double-doors down the white hallway. "Having warp technology is a big deal to them. Interstellar travel gives them, well..." She stopped and just shrugged.

What it gave them, Harr knew, was a chance at space battle. Not all military personnel were battle-hungry, but it seemed that most military complexes were. Harr thought back to the numerous commanding officers he'd had over the years. More than one should never have risen in the ranks at all—Admiral Parfait came to mind. Most got to the top because they had no qualms about stepping on the heads of others. Of course that could be said about essentially any industry. Regardless, if the military was stationed in the building, he'd have to stay on his toes.

"Obviously they'd be interested, yes," Harr said. "Makes total sense."

"Yes," said DeKella, touching her badge to the lock plate. A click and buzz sounded and she pushed on through. "Warp technology is still in its infancy, but if our test succeeds we'll be one step closer to visiting distant galaxies."

"Yes, I know how it is to…" Harr started and then caught himself. "I mean, who on Kallian doesn't know about the famous warp test, right?"

"You're right, of course!" DeKella stopped and looked at Harr. "I didn't mean to sound patronizing."

"No, you didn't," Harr said quickly. "I was just…I mean, I probably said the wrong…"

"It was clearly my doing," DeKella said.

"No, really, I…"

"Maybe we should get to work?" Vool interrupted.

"Right," Harr said with a sigh. "Sorry, Dr. Piffer is a stickler."

"And you're an asshole," Vool stated.

"Wow," DeKella said. "That was pretty direct."

Harr was staring laser-beams at Vool, though she didn't seem to care. "Don't mind Dr. Piffer," he said tightly, "she has issues with saying things aloud. Can't be helped. Sometimes she even suggests to people that she has a desire to kill them. One can only assume it to be a medical condition of some sort."

"Oh, I see," DeKella said gently as she focused on Vool. "That's very sad. Is there nothing that would help with your situation?"

"Killing you might help," Vool suggested.

"See what I mean?" said Harr, grabbing DeKella by the

elbow. "Maybe we should just move along. She only gets worse if you keep pressing the issue."

DeKella glanced down at her elbow and then gave Harr an interested look. He immediately let go, feeling a fool. She smiled and then continued walking down the corridor.

"Right, well, this is the main floor for the W.A.R.P.E.D. building. As the guard had said, there are floors upstairs that we won't be covering, but everything you'll be interested in is on the lower levels anyway." She motioned toward a number of pictures that hung on the wall. Each had names of doctors stenciled underneath. "We've been doing research on the current project for roughly twenty years here. These are the past heads of the project. This last one is me, obviously. I've been in charge here for five years now. That happened because I found the key to the *Garvel Paradox*." She peered back over her shoulder. "I'm assuming you know about this paradox?"

"No," Ridly chimed in before Harr could answer.

DeKella turned toward Ridly and seemed to glow.

"It's quite fascinating," she said excitedly. "Dr. Blathe Garvel, a renowned physicist, suggested that if we were to fold space and travel in an instant from one location to another, we would likely leave traces of ourselves on both sides. This would mean that we would never be fully present in either location, meaning that we would simultaneously perish in both locations. The famous example that he used was to take a fountain pen and draw a smiley face at the top of a piece of paper. Then, without waiting for the ink to dry, he folded the paper in two and rubbed it around a bit. When he unfolded it, there were two face-like smudges on each side. This, Dr. Garvel decided, proved his theory."

"Ah," said a confused-looking Ridly.

"That makes very little sense," Vool stated with a grunt, "and it's not even a paradox."

"That's precisely what I thought," DeKella replied with a nod. "You have to understand, though, that back in Dr. Garvel's day, there weren't many physicists, so people tended to believe just about anything they said. Anyway," she continued, "after doing much research I stumbled upon another scientist of the day, a Dr. Paul McCarthy, who said that Dr. Garvel's theory was complete idiocy. The problem was that Dr. McCarthy was a psychologist, not a physicist, so they discounted his ideas as being mental poppycock." She giggled a little at this. "Well, it turns out that Dr. McCarthy's ideas on the subject were fascinating. He showed that by using a ballpoint pen that has no smear qualities, and by placing a film of thin plastic over the page prior to bending it, one could fold the paper and smudge all they want with zero impact or trace elements."

"Interesting," Ridly said after a few moments, "but that doesn't get the image from one side of the page to the other."

"Well done, Dr. Baloo," DeKella declared with a clap of her hands. "But, you see, Dr. McCarthy didn't stop there. He decided that if the goal was to move the image from one folded half of the page to the other, all one would need to do is cut the image out and tape it to the other side." She let that sink in. "It's a brilliant solution to the problem. So much so that I ended up pushing for it to be recognized by the scientific community. After much convincing, my fellow physicists began to see the merit in Dr. McCarthy's work. The theory was adopted, named the *McCarthy Snip-n-Tape Equation*, and an award was given to his descendants in his memory. Since I was the one who discovered this amazing work, and brought it to the next level, I was asked to run the warp test."

Harr scanned the rest of the crew. Their faces all held the same gaze he was certain his face held: confusion.

"I don't get it," he said. "How does the *McCarthy Cut-n-Paste*..."

"*Snip-n-Tape*," DeKella corrected.

"Right, sorry, so how does the *McCarthy Snip-n-Tape*, which was supposed to be used for folding space-time, play a role in warp technology?"

"The tape part," she said as if that explained everything. She then obviously saw that it did not. "If you take a piece of paper and wrap tape around it, it becomes outside of space-time."

"It does?" asked Ridly.

"In the test, yes," said DeKella. "Not in real life. That would be absurd."

"Everything about this conversation has been absurd," Vool said. "Not to mention boring."

"Okay, Dr. Piffer," Harr said warningly. "Sorry, Dr. DeKella. Please go on."

"Well, by using the *McCarthy Snip-n-Tape Equation*, I was able to look beyond the page-folding since everyone knows that instantaneous travel is impossible."

"Actually..." Jezden began.

"Let her finish, Dr. Impotent," Harr said with a sharp glance.

"Oh yeah," Jezden said, clearly catching himself. "My bad."

"Anyway," she continued, "instantaneous travel is about as likely as making things like, say, cloaking or time-travel work, so I decided to try something different. If I put an element inside of the metaphorical 'tape,' I can have it zip through space without so much as a how-do-ya-do!"

"Huh," Harr said, shocked that he, a common soldier, knew more about the basics of physics than a high-ranking doctor on the lonely world of Kallian. "That's truly...fascinating."

"It is, isn't it?" she said, this time dragging Harr by the

elbow. "Anyway, I could go on for hours, but we have work to do. Now, over here is the cafeteria, in case you have any late-night cravings. They have great sandwiches, but watch out for the soup. It's been known to make some men impotent." She turned toward Jezden in a flash. "I'm terribly sorry, doctor, but it's the truth. I'm not trying to be insensitive to your problem."

"What problem?" Jezden said hotly. "Just because my name is 'Impotent,' doesn't mean my junk is." He waved his hands around his groin and added, "Everything down here is working just fine, thank you very much."

"I…uh…"

"Forget about it, Dr. DeKella," Harr said. "He's just a bit sensitive. You know how small-tails are."

"Ha, ha, ha," Jezden said, sneering. "Live it up, Captain. You finally have something on you bigger than…"

"Dr. DeKella," Ridly said, interrupting Jezden's tirade, "are we close to the main lab? I'd like to get a first-hand look at the machinery. We don't have much time left, you know."

"Yes, of course," DeKella said after a moment. "It's on minus-three. We keep it underground in the event that something goes wrong." She turned white. "Not that we expect anything to go wrong, of course. It's just that we wanted to take every precaution. I don't want you to think that *we* expect anything bad to happen. We don't. We're very confident…"

"I understand," Ridly said reassuringly. "These types of tests can greatly impact society. We hope for a positive outcome, but we prepare for the negative. As Dr. Welder said before, we're here to help minimize the negative. Having the test happen underground is a wise decision, and that is a point in your favor."

"Thank you," DeKella said sincerely. "And we're truly glad you're all here to help. For once, I actually think I mean that."

The lift was very odd-looking indeed. It was in the shape of a decagon, with black padded rectangles mounted to each of the ten slats. There were metallic claws folded open beside the pads. Harr assumed that they were used to restrain passengers.

"Are any of you susceptible to motion sickness?"

Ridly and Jezden pointed at Harr. They were obviously referring to the bouncing around of the *Reluctant* during their space battle a couple of days prior. He rolled his eyes.

"That was just an isolated event. I'll be fine."

"Are you sure?" DeKella said. "The lift is very fast and moves both horizontally and vertically. It can be rather jarring."

"I'm certain," Harr said, "but thank you for your concern."

"All right, you'll want to press your backs against one of the pads, get comfortable and then press the button that you'll feel near your right hand."

Harr did as he was told. The claws slowly closed in on him until they were pressing him firmly into the pad. It wasn't exactly uncomfortable, but he did feel a hint of claustrophobia. It would be over soon enough, he told himself. Obviously these people did this all the time, so there was nothing to worry about.

"Now, once we start moving, the claws will tighten and loosen a bit. This is to compensate for the motion. Don't worry, though. A group of inspectors such as yourselves spent three days evaluating this system. There was only one death and that was because one of the testers wanted to see how the lift managed without the restraints. Due to the results of that particular test, there is now a failsafe that won't allow the lift to move unless everyone is properly strapped in." Once they were secured, Dr. DeKella said, "Lift, take us to minus-3, please."

"Acknowledged," replied a voice that made Geezer sound updated. "Transfer commencing in three...two...one..."

The jolt was so strong that Harr felt like his knees were going to pop out of his skull. The instant that he started to acclimate to the drop, the lift bolted left, making his innards slide to the right. Then it dropped again, stopped, rotated, lifted, cut right, and dropped again.

Finally, after what felt like an eternity, it came to a halt and Harr threw up all over the place.

"Told ya," Jezden said.

THE KALLIAN COMMANDER

*G*eneral Struggins stood behind a one-way glass pane that overlooked the warp-lab floor. From his perch, he could see all of the goings on, but nobody could see him. Scientists were a predictable bunch. They spent most of their days actually working on things that they were supposed to be working on. In the 17 months that he'd been stationed here, not a single thing had been deemed suspicious.

And then the inspectors had arrived. He'd known that they were coming, of course. It was the way of things. But it irked him to no end that he didn't have a clue regarding their identities. Who in their right mind thought that it made sense to hide information regarding someone with the power to stop an entire operation such as this in its tracks?

There were four of them. Two male, two female. Well, one of the males had such a short tail that his gender was questionable. Were it not for the obvious muscle tone and strong jawbone, he would have had to wonder.

"Deddles," he called out to the private who had entered the room, "what do you know about these inspectors?"

Deddles rushed across the room and saluted. "Only that they are inspectors, sir."

"I know that much, Deddles. *Everyone* knows that much."

"Yes, sir," Deddles replied in his squeaky voice. "We never get details regarding inspectors, sir. That would be against regulations. They are very concerned over being compromised through bribery or something."

"I know how the process works, Private," Struggins said tersely. "My point is that we're in the military. We have access to things that others do not." He glanced questioningly at Deddles. "You get where I'm going with this?"

"I think so, sir," Deddles answered, "but just to be sure... are you asking me to look into their records, sir?"

Struggins leaned backward, putting on his best affronted look. "Heavens no, Deddles. I'm not asking you anything of the sort." He scoffed a couple of times before looking back down on the figures in the lab. "I'm merely suggesting that an enterprising young private who has an interest in moving up the military chain of command might find his way more clear were he to be forward-thinking."

The military had changed greatly since Struggins was a private. There was a time where soldiers did what they had to do, regardless of the consequences. It was how you got noticed. You'd end up with a slap across the wrist now and again, but it was always under the guise of a proud superior officer who knew that you were just playing the game. Today's entry class was all about doing the right thing, the ethical thing. To Struggins' way of thinking, the only right and ethical decisions a soldier had to worry about were the ones that furthered the power of the Kallian forces.

"So," Deddles said, looking unsure, "should I look into their records, sir?"

"Private Deddles," Struggins said with a sigh, "I have made

no such request of you, nor have I commanded you thusly. Are we clear about that?"

"I think so, sir."

"You *think* so?"

"Well, it's just…"

"I'll help you be completely certain, Private," Struggins said, raising his voice from its standard grumble to that of a subdued drill sergeant. "I am formally stating that I am in no way, shape, or form giving you any direction whatsoever that would lead you to conclude that you should look up the records for any of these inspectors. Do you understand me, Private?"

"Yes, sir!"

"Good," Struggins said, relaxing. He let the heat settle for a moment, looking around to make sure that everyone else in the room was busily working on their assigned tasks. Then he lowered his voice and said, "Are you planning to be a private all of your life, son?"

"No, sir."

"Can you imagine yourself holding the rank of someone as lofty as myself?"

"It would be a dream come true, sir."

"Do you know how I got to this position, Deddles?"

"Looking at inspectors' records, sir?"

"Precisely," Struggins said and then turned sharply toward the private. "Wait, no, not that."

"Oh," Deddles said. "Um, hard work and determination then, sir?"

"I got here, Private, by taking risks." He gripped his hands behind his back, pushing his chest out so that his medals were more impressive. "I bent the rules when they needed bending, and I took initiative to do the things that needed to be done so that our wonderful military establishment moved in the most fitting direction for the survival of our people and our planet."

"Yes, sir."

"I did not get here by simply waiting around to be told what to do."

"No, sir."

"Are you understanding my meaning here, Private?"

"I need to take risks, sir," Deddles said, standing at attention and speaking firmly, but keeping his voice low enough to match how Struggins had been talking. "I need to bend the rules where they need bending, and I need to do the things that need doing in order to help our military establishment move in the direction most fitting for its goals, sir."

"Well done, Deddles," Struggins said, surprised at the boy's grasp of the situation. "Now, I plan to ask you again at some point today what we know about our inspectors down there. When I ask you this question again, Private Deddles, do you suppose you will have a more informative response for me?"

Private Deddles looked like a man who had seen breasts for the first time. "Yes, sir. I will, sir."

"There's a good soldier."

THE LAB

*T*hey had spent the better part of an hour going through the various pieces of technology that filled the lab.

Ridly was the only one who seemed to really understand what was going on, but Harr did his best to nod as knowingly as possible whenever the opportunity came up. Vool was continuously scanning the area. She clearly had something nefarious up her sleeve. Jezden was more useless than usual. There wasn't a female scientist within the vastness of the lab who hadn't snickered at the length of the android's tail. There also wasn't one that hadn't given Harr an appraising glance regarding the length of his.

"…and this," DeKella said as she pointed toward an enormous ball-shaped hunk of metal, "is the Multicombo Chamber. This is where all the magic happens."

"Can you explain?" Harr asked.

"Of course, Dr. Welder. If you follow the direction of this pipe, you'll see that it connects to the room up those stairs. Inside that room there is another orb that's about one-quarter the size of this one. It's where we house the

Stewnathium Particles that will be poured into this chamber during the test." She took a quick sip of water. "Once the particles fill the Multicombo Chamber, along with a mixture of other particles, they will merge in a dance of electrical mayhem. As soon as their combination is complete, which will take a fraction of a second from our perspective, a dense magnetic field will begin to form."

Harr couldn't help but notice how excited Dr. DeKella was about this topic. It was clear that her entire life had been building to this point. He felt terrible that it would all come crashing down around her shoulders, but it was either that or the extinction of the Kallian species...not to mention himself and the crew of the *SSMC Reluctant*.

"Now," she continued, "when that magnetic field kicks in, we take it and focus it around an object. The power of the field will begin to warp the space around said item—my metaphorical piece of tape. That's what we call a 'warp bubble,' and it's the thing that will allow the object to move freely in a perceived velocity that exceeds the speed of light."

"Could you expand on that a little more?" asked Ridly, seeming to be genuinely interested.

"Think of it like being on a wave in the ocean," DeKella explained. "You're on top of the wave and it's moving at a very fast speed. Now, imagine that it doesn't come crashing down. Instead, it starts way out in the middle of the sea and it rushes along, unfettered, for hundreds of miles. While you sit on the top of that wave, you're going to be moving very quickly, but everything around that wave will be moving at the rate it always moves, except for maybe a bit of a jolting that will be fleeting, at best. Does that make sense?"

"No," Vool stated. "It's complete idiocy."

Dr. DeKella gawked at Harr, who merely shrugged and rolled his eyes. "Right," she said, "well, now we take that same oceanic description and stick it in space. We can then imagine riding a wave in space, but this wave allows us to zoom around faster than light while not violating the laws of Quenstein's *Theory of Geriatric Relations.*"

"Sorry," Ridly said, "don't you mean the *Theory of General Relativity?*"

"I've never heard of that," said DeKella with a faraway look. "Was that one of Quenstein's theories?"

"No," Harr stated before Ridly could reply. "Different guy completely. Not really related. Could you refresh us on *Geriatric Relations?*"

"Really?" she said while scrunching her face.

"Please."

"I would imagine it's the same as when younger people have relations. More wrinkly, I suppose, and they probably require blue pills and better lubrication, but…"

"No, sorry," Harr interrupted before things got out of hand, especially with Jezden being within earshot. "Not geriatric relations in general, Doctor. I meant specifically Quenstein's *Theory of Geriatric Relations.*"

"Oh, right!" She shook her head, turning a bit red in the process. "How silly of me. I thought that you actually wanted me to explain…" She glanced up at Harr. "Sorry. Quenstein's *Theory of Geriatric Relations* states that when you approach the speed of light, you get old really fast."

"Uh," Ridly started, "I don't think…"

"Ah, yes," Harr interrupted, "first year stuff at the university. Slipped my mind. Maybe," Harr joked lamely, "I've been moving too close to the speed of light." Nobody laughed. "You know, getting old, losing my memory. Never mind."

Dr. DeKella leaned on the Multicombo Chamber. "Are there any other questions?"

"What happens if the *Stewnathium Particles* don't make it to the core?" asked Ridly.

"Excellent question, Dr. Baloo. It's simple, really. No particles, no warp field. They are a key component in the mix, and are part of the mathematical solution I put together to solve the problem in the first place. In essence, I discovered the *Stewnathium Particles*."

"If that's true," said Jezden, "then why aren't they named the *DeKella Particles?*"

"I considered it, Dr. Impotent," DeKella said. "After a lot of thought, though, I had to admit that the mathematical side of my work was largely based on the proofs of Dr. Stewnathium—may he rest in peace—and so I felt that he should receive the lion's share of the credit."

"Oh, yeah," Jezden said, "forgot about good old Dr. Stewnathium."

"I'm surprised you've even heard of him, Dr. Impotent. He was never exactly famous. Well, at least not until now."

"You have to remember, Dr. DeKella," Ridly said with an evil grin, "Dr. Impotent has a lot of time to study about obscure things, what with his small tail and all."

"I suppose that's true," DeKella said. "Sorry, Dr. Impotent."

Jezden grunted and moved away from the group. Harr found it challenging to feel bad for the guy. Yes, it wasn't really the android's fault that he was such a tool, being that he was programmed to be as such, but Harr knew that these "learning androids" could improve themselves if they wanted to. Jezden had simply never wanted to.

"So, Dr. DeKella," said Harr, "as long as these particles make it through, and the proper mix of other elements is in that chamber, you expect that the field will work?"

"Unless my calculations are wrong, Dr. Welder, it should work perfectly."

"You know what that means, Welder," Vool said sinisterly.

"Yes, Dr. Piffer, I do. It means that we need to get to work testing things around here to make sure that this facility meets all necessary safety regulations."

"And you'll have complete autonomy to do so," DeKella said emphatically. "The only thing that I ask is that you make sure someone is with you if you want to run any particular machinery."

"You mean there are no testing documents available?" asked Ridly.

"Not precisely, no. There just hasn't been time. However," she said, reaching behind the chamber and pulling out a thick book, "each section has a procedural manual. If you follow the instructions step-by-step, things should work out just fine, but seeing that our primary focus was to get the test ready in time, our documentation is admittedly dated."

"Sounds like an immediate fail to me," Vool stated. "I'll contact Veli and get the wheels in motion."

"Finally," Harr said with a chuckle, "Dr. Piffer makes a joke. Good one, Dr. Piffer."

"I wasn't joking."

"Aha, and yet another attempt at pulling the old leg, as it were. That dry humor of yours is something to behold."

"You're being obtuse, Harr."

"Harr?" said DeKella with her eyebrows raised.

"Harr…harr…harr," said Harr. "She only laughs in single syllables."

"I wasn't…"

"Dr. Baloo," Harr said quickly, "why don't you and the other two doctors start introducing yourselves around?" He leaned in close to Ridly. "And stick together."

"Yes, right," Ridly said. "That's an excellent idea, Dr. Welder."

Ridly pulled Vool and Jezden along, going from station to station. As they set about getting acquainted with the

W.A.R.P.E.D. test team, Harr tried to make sure DeKella was kept relaxed about their presence.

"Don't mind her," he said with a casual wave. "She's been this odd since the day I met her."

"That's okay. I get a lot of strange people in my group. Being smart often comes with its fair share of social quirks."

"Indeed, it does."

There was an awkward pause before DeKella said, "Is there anything else you may need from me before I get back to work? I have a lot on my plate, as you know."

"No, nothing at all," Harr said understandingly. "We've got a lot of work to do as well."

"I hope it all goes smoothly, but please let me know if you spot anything out of place and we will address it immediately."

"Absolutely, yes," said Harr, not wanting the conversation to end but realizing it was inevitable. "It's been really nice meeting you, Dr. DeKella. I mean, I think you're great." He slammed his eyes shut, disbelieving he'd just said that. "That is to say that I've read a lot about you and I think that you're a pretty amazing person." That wasn't any better.

"How very kind of you to say, Dr. Welder," she replied with a smile, putting her hand on his arm.

"Call me Don," Harr replied without thought.

"Don?"

"Zep! I mean, Zep. Don is my, uh, middle name. Some people call me that, but, anyway, just call me Zep."

"Okay, Zep it is," she replied. "You can call me Rella." She turned and began walking away, but stopped and turned back. "Zep, would you like to go to dinner with me tonight?"

"Uh…"

"It'll be strictly professional," she said as if catching herself. "I mean, if you don't feel that we should…"

"Yes," Harr replied, stopping her before she freaked out, "that would be nice."

"Great. Uh, there's a nice restaurant across from the hotel we're setting you and your team up in. What say we meet there around seven?"

"Seven it is."

Harr watched her walk down the corridor. Once she turned the corner, he took a deep breath and wished that they were meeting under different circumstances. Everything he was about to do was ultimately for the benefit of the Kallian people, including Dr. DeKella, but he had a feeling she wasn't going to see it that way. He supposed that it was better she hated him and lived, than liked him and died.

When he turned to check on the rest of the crew, he found Vool had been standing directly behind him. It was all he could do not to jump.

"You're not getting involved with that woman, are you?" she asked pointedly.

"Of course not. I'm simply playing my part in this charade just like the rest of you."

"Somehow I doubt that."

"Fortunately, what you think has little bearing on anything, Vool," Harr said. "You were specifically ordered by Frexle to observe only."

"And judge, Harr."

"That's another thing," Harr said, ignoring her point about judging their actions, "get my name right in front of the Kallians. If we fail, it needs to be on us and not due to the mistake of a supposedly uber-intelligent Overseer."

JUST A SAYING

Frexle couldn't recall a project that had landed him in the Lord Overseer's office more than this one. There had been one plan that had pitted two major continents on Rembar-19 against each other that Veli had seemed exceedingly interested in. The Rembar-19 incident had ended with a light show that all but split the planet in two. Amazingly, people had survived and, after many years of nomadic living, began making a comeback. Veli had expressed hope that they would again rise to the point of bringing him another glorious display of antics. During that project, Veli had summoned Frexle four times in five days, and Frexle had considered that extreme.

"They have to be on that damned planet by now," Veli more spat than spoke. "Why hasn't that infernal Vool reported anything yet?"

"Maybe she's tied up, Lord Overseer," Frexle replied.

Veli's voice grew dark. "You think those Kallian bastards have somehow managed to take her captive?"

"Sorry, sir," Frexle said, recalling that the Lord Overseer was not all that keen on sayings, "it's just a saying."

"My office is no place for that kind of speak, Frexle," Veli growled. "We've had this discussion before. Speak straight or find yourself floating in space like a leaf on a river."

Frexle had just begun to bow his head apologetically when the phone rang.

"Where in blazes have you been, Vool?" Veli said as the face of Vool showed up on the video display that sat on the wall. "We've been waiting hours to hear about your progress."

"I was tied up," she replied curtly.

"So they *did* capture you," Veli said with a hiss.

"No," she replied. "It's just a saying."

Veli groaned and slammed his desk. "Just tell me what is happening. The last I heard from you was when you were on that damned ship. I want details. Leave nothing to spare."

"Okay," Vool said resignedly. "First we landed on the planet and Harr started to hand out our badges. I ended up as a Dr. Piffer or something. Harr is Dr. Welder, Ridly is Baloo, and Jezden is Impotent."

"Oh, that's too bad," Veli said. "Wouldn't wish that on anyone."

"Horrible," Frexle agreed.

"Next we stepped off the ship and started walking through the park, and…"

"Vool," Veli interrupted, "I don't need that much information."

"You said not to spare any details."

"I was using a say…well, never mind. Just give me the pertinent data."

Vool rolled her eyes. "Fine. We just got back from the lab. It seems that there's a chance to stop this test from succeeding. All Harr and his crew have to do is block these things called *Stewnathium Particles* from getting to the main chamber. They do that and it'll look like a flop."

"Damn," Veli said. "If Harr succeeds, there'll be no killings."

Frexle sat up and furrowed his brow. "That's what we want, though, right, sir?"

"No, Frexle, that's what the *people* want." Veli did seem to enjoy speaking in italics when things got heated. "Or, at least, that's what they *think* they want. But what do they know?"

"I still expect them to fail," Vool said before Frexle could counter. "They're not very bright."

"Underestimation is a *deadly* game, Vool," warned Veli, "even for an Overseer. Remember that they have survived this far."

"Whatever."

"We need to make sure that they don't succeed."

"You're talking about the Kallians, sir?"

"Of course not, Frexle. I'm talking about this Platoon F of yours."

"Sir?"

"Wait," Veli said, clearly ignoring Frexle's concerns, "I've got it. Vool, if we set this up right, the people will see that we *tried* to be kinder and gentler, but it just didn't work out. They'll see that we did what we could to avoid outright destruction. Sadly, this new crew that we—no, that *Frexle* brought to us—failed miserably."

Frexle bolted from his chair, momentarily losing his senses. It wasn't wise to move so quickly around the Lord Overseer. Every automated weapon in the room spun and focused in on Frexle so quickly that he thought certain he was a goner. He stayed perfectly still until Veli told the guns to stand down.

"Thank you, sir," Frexle said with relief, "but to pin this on me without even giving them…"

"It *was* your idea, wasn't it, Frexle?"

"Well, yes," Frexle admitted. "But, sir, they can succeed."

"Not if we stop them," Veli replied sinisterly. "And the people will be none the wiser. They'll only hear how we gave it our best shot. Oh, how we had such high hopes for this team of yours," Veli said in a mocking voice. "Sadly, they just couldn't deliver."

"I'm stunned," said Frexle, feeling stunned.

"At my genius? I can understand that." He paused as Frexle let the ordeal sink in. "You'll have to take the fall, Frexle. It's what *good* leaders do, after all. But don't you worry, I'll make sure your death is quick."

"I don't believe this is happening," Frexle said in a near whisper.

"Anyone else finding this conversation to be dull?" Vool piped in. "What do you want me to do?"

"Ah, yes," Veli said, sounding rather chipper indeed. "I want you to place explosives in that room, Vool. The moment the Kallians press the button, I want you to activate those explosives."

"That will only blow up the building," Vool noted.

"Not if you use the proper kind of explosives, Vool," Veli replied with dripping evil.

Vool smiled seductively. "Finally showing some balls, Veli."

"I am?" There was a shuffling sound in the shadows.

"Just a saying," Vool replied with a sigh.

"Oh, right."

CHECKING WITH GEEZER

*I*t had been a long day working at the lab, so Harr was pleased to have gotten over to the hotel that Dr. DeKella's assistant had arranged for them. All four rooms were on the same floor, with Harr's being a suite at the corner.

The life of an inspector was comfortable indeed, assuming this was the norm. Even on Harr's best vacation, he'd never gotten digs this plush. Currently he was sitting in a large chair that was leaned back, allowing him to sink nicely into its burgundy leather embrace.

Jezden and Ridly were on the couch opposite him. He'd invited them over to his room so that they could compare notes without Vool being around. He'd also called Geezer in on the conversation and had him on speaker.

Ridly was busily running through her day of work. She had gotten into the spirit of things during the inspection, finding a number of issues that were all addressed by Dr. DeKella's team. Had Harr not known better, he would have assumed that Ridly actually *was* an inspector. To be fair, she was programmed to have that way of thinking.

Jezden, however, mostly moped around, trying one-liners on every Kallian female he could find. None of them responded kindly. Looks or not, on Kallian a tail made the person. He was still rather depressed as he sat on the couch, gazing out the window.

"It's actually a pretty interesting piece of technology, Geezer," Harr was saying into his wristband. "I think you'd find it fascinating."

"Can it do instantaneous travel, chief?"

"Well, no."

"Time travel?"

"Not that I'm aware," he answered, looking up at Ridly who shook her head to indicate the negative.

"So it's old hat, big dog," Geezer replied snootily.

"Compared to what we do, sure, but it's the top of the line on this planet."

"Sorry, honcho, but if it ain't the latest, then it ain't the greatest."

"No offense, Geezer, but you're not exactly the latest either."

"Ouch," Geezer replied. "How am I not supposed to take offense to that one, cap'n?"

"Sorry," Harr said after a few seconds. "That was uncalled for. I guess I'm just…"

Jezden stood up and said, "He's got the hots for DeKella" as he walked to the window. "Not my type, but on this planet it seems I'm nobody's type, so more power to you."

"What are you talking about?" Harr said in disbelief.

"Oh, I see how it is," Geezer said. "The scientist lady's got you all wrapped up, eh? Good for you, prime."

Harr adjusted uncomfortably in his seat. There was no hiding the fact that Dr. DeKella was pleasant to look at, and she had a mind that was considered one of the greatest on this entire planet. Granted, that wasn't saying much when compared to the minds of other, more advanced, planets, but here, she was up there. Plus, she was kind and somewhat geeky. He liked that in a woman.

"I'm interested in her in a strictly professional manner, I assure you," he said carefully.

"Come on, Captain," Jezden scoffed. "Own up, already. You're talking to a player here."

"You're not a player on this planet, small tail," Harr spat back.

"Ouch."

"Damn." He slapped himself on the forehead. "I did it again. I'm sorry, Ensign. I don't know what's gotten into me."

"Love?" suggested Ridly.

"Oh please, don't make me sick," said Jezden.

"Lust, then?"

"What? No!" Harr grimaced at her. Then he sat back again and dropped his head. "Okay, possibly that, and a great deal of like, too. What can I say? She's kinda hot."

"Sir," said Sandoo, who was obviously standing with Geezer in the *Reluctant's* engineering room, "I appreciate your position there, but it's my duty to remind you that your first duty is to the crew."

"It's always my first duty, Commander," Harr replied before deciding to change the subject. "Enough about me. What have you found about Vool?"

"According to the tracking device we've got on her tail," Sandoo answered, "she left her quarters about five minutes ago. She's just entered the W.A.R.P.E.D. building."

Harr shook his head. "Why didn't you say something before?"

"Because," Sandoo answered, "we were busily discussing your love life, sir."

If only there were other actual humans around, he thought. No, that would probably be worse. At least the androids responded in a programmatic way. Real humans could be much more aggravating.

"Can you see what she's seeing?" he asked.

"Yes, sir. We're keeping close tabs on everything she does."

"Make sure you do," said Harr, taking a quick peek at the clock. "Damn, it's almost seven already." He pushed up out of the chair with a groan. It was extremely comfortable. "I have to run. Sandoo, Ridly and Jezden will work with you and Geezer to figure things out, should Vool do anything untoward." He stopped at the door. "And believe me, she's planning to do something untoward."

"Yes, sir."

"Hey, Bingo," Geezer said, "one more thing before you leave."

"Yes?"

"Make sure you wear protection."

GOOD TIMES LEEKO'S

The walk across the street was much calmer at this time of night. Nobody called him names and the pushing and shoving had all but disappeared.

Good Times Leeko's was the name of the restaurant. It was your standard-looking joint, though possibly on the higher-end of the financial scale, and that was only a guess since the clientele wore mostly suits. Harr felt a tad underdressed in comparison, but there wasn't much he could do about that.

He approached the host, who held up a finger as he finished writing something down. "Done," he said with a grunt before throwing the pen down. "Table for one?"

"Uh, no, I'm meeting someone."

"Name?"

"Don Harr...erm, I mean, huh? What was that?"

"Your name, sir?" the host asked more loudly.

"Ah, right. Dr. Zep Welder."

The host scanned the list and then nodded. "You're meeting Dr. DeKella. This way, please."

They walked a lazy path through the bustling restaurant.

Laughter filled the room, as did many bottles of alcohol, which Harr knew to be the case because his HUD (Heads-Up Display) kept showing him the ingredients of everything. Sensory overload was an understatement. He forced himself to focus on ignoring the data until they finally arrived at the booth where Dr. DeKella was seated. Her glass was full of fermented grapes.

"Thank you," he said to the host and then took the seat across from DeKella. "Hello, Doctor...sorry, Rella. I hope I'm not too late."

"Not at all," she replied with a smile that said this was not her first glass of wine. "I've been here for a little while, but I always show up far earlier than I need to. Trying to make up for my chronic lateness when in college, I suppose." She took another sip. "Have you eaten here before?"

"No," he said. "I've never even been to your planet...erm, play net...play network?" He groaned. "I've never been to your city."

"You're an odd one, Zep," she said with a wan smile. "I like that in a man."

"Thanks?"

She swirled her drink in the glass. "What city are you from?"

"Uh, well, let's see," he said. "How do I answer that?"

"Wait, wait, wait," DeKella said with a start, setting her glass back on the table. "I'm terribly sorry. I forgot that you're not allowed to provide those types of details. At least not while you're engaged in the inspections."

"Right," Harr replied with a sense of relief. "Exactly."

She pushed the drink away. "We should just stick to business."

"Or we could talk about you," Harr suggested.

"Me?"

"Sure. I'd love to hear more about you. Where you grew

up, the schools you attended, how you got into science... everything." She seemed perplexed. "It'll help me put together a picture of you for testing. If I understand your perspective on things, I can make better judgment calls."

"That's fascinating," she replied, leaning in. "I hadn't considered that before. Actually, let me write that down." She pulled out an electronic pad and started to scribble something with her fingertip. "There, got it."

Just as she'd set down the pad, the waitress came up to the table. She held a sneer that marked her as someone who obviously wanted to just collect her pay and go home. Harr glanced around at the other wait staff and noted they all appeared that way.

"Whaddya wanna drink?" she said.

"Um," Harr said, not knowing the options, "I guess I'll just have what she's having."

Both women gawked at him. "Really?" they said in unison.

"I take it there's something wrong with that?"

The waitress scoffed and said, "Only that it's from the female side of the menu."

"The female side?" said Harr with a grimace.

"Where are you from, buddy, the moon?"

She flipped open the menu and pointed at it. Sure enough there were two columns. Male and Female. Jezden would have approved. Interestingly, the items on the female side were far more expensive than those on the male side.

"Sorry," Harr said. "I'm not from your country. Just give me the male version of what she's having." The waitress rolled her eyes, grunted, and then walked away. "Well, that'll be reflected in her tip."

"Tip?" said DeKella.

"Yes," Harr answered and then gazed up to see that she didn't know what he was talking about. They'd probably just had another word for it on Kallian. "You know, extra money for doing a good job."

DeKella picked up her pad again. "I've never heard of such a thing. Most of the time wait staff is abysmal." She tapped a couple of times on the pad and then her eyes lit up. "So, what you're saying is that if you gave them some incentive, maybe they wouldn't be such jerks?"

"Works where I'm from," he said with a shrug. "Most of the time, anyway."

He studied the menu, noting items from the men's side having names such as *Steak Kablam* and *Dire Bird with Green Stalks*. Following across to the women's side, the same options were named *Flowered Beef* and *Lavender Poultry with Emerald Veggies*. He allowed himself to see the ingredients list on his HUD. They were identical. Very odd.

"Interesting menu," he said. "Any suggestions?"

"My husband usually gets the *Gurgling Shark*, if that helps?"

"Husband?" said Harr, feeling his heart sink.

"We're in the middle of a conscious uncoupling."

"What?"

"Divorce."

"Oh, that's good," he said and then coughed. "Sorry! I mean, that's awful. I'm sorry to hear it."

"No, it *is* good," she said with a laugh. "It was bound to happen eventually. He's a businessman and I'm a scientist. The only thing we had in common was the length of our tails."

"I see."

"Sex solves a lot of problems on Kallian," she said while picking up her wine glass again, "but not everything." She drank deeply this time, then she tilted her head and said, "Your tail is a fair bit longer than his."

Harr felt himself blush. He still had little idea what one's tail signified. If she expected it meant that he had an equally sized *other side*, she would be sorely disappointed were the evening to turn out the way he'd hoped.

"That was probably inappropriate for your area of the world," DeKella said after a moment. She closed her eyes and dropped her head. "I'm sorry if I've offended you. I've never been good at drinking. The stress of the day…"

"No, it's okay," said Harr. "We say things like that where I come from, too. It just usually takes a little while of getting to know someone first."

"You mean like a courting period?"

"That's about right, yes."

"Interesting."

"Well," Harr said, "we just don't want to offend anyone."

"I guess because I grew up here, I can't comprehend how someone could be offended by hearing that you find something attractive about their person."

Harr went to respond, but then realized she'd had a point. "Actually, I suppose they shouldn't be, but that's just the way of things in some cultures, I suppose."

"I can't see how anyone would. Who doesn't like to hear nice things about themselves?"

"Masochists?"

"Fair enough," she said. "Well, you're in my land now, so tell me something that you find attractive about…me."

"Seriously?" he said with a nervous laugh.

"Unless you find nothing attractive about me, of course."

"On the contrary," Harr said, leaning back in this chair. "Okay, here goes…you've got great breasts."

"Breasts?" she said as if slapped. "Who cares about breasts?"

Harr frowned. "I guess I do."

"Are you one of those kinky types, Zep?" she asked after a moment.

"If liking breasts makes me kinky," he replied, folding his arms, "then I suppose I am."

"Fair enough. Fair enough." She laughed and shook her head. "I guess it could be worse. You could have said I had nice legs."

"Yes," Harr said out of the corner of his mouth, "that would be...worse. So what kind of things do you find attractive, Rella?"

"Besides tails, you mean?"

"Well, yeah."

"Just the standard things," she said while waving her hand. "Toenails, eyelids, ear hair, the little webbing of skin where the thumb meets the forefinger." She must have noticed the look on Harr's face because she added, "I assume that's all pretty dull to a man who likes breasts."

"Not at all," he said, even though it was weird in his estimation. "It's just different than what I'm used to."

Thankfully, the waitress returned before the conversation could go much deeper. She set his drink down and then just stood there with her hands on her hips, looking expectantly at Harr and DeKella. She was even chewing gum, or some gum-like substance anyway, and she wasn't exactly going out of her way to hide that fact.

"Well," she said to Harr, "whaddya want?"

Harr motioned toward DeKella who replied with, "Gentlemen first."

"Uh, okay." Kallian was completely backward from what he was used to. "I guess I'll have the *Gurgling Shark*."

"How do you want it cooked?"

"I'll just take it however most people take it."

The waitress sighed. "Most people take it however they want it cooked."

"Excuse me," DeKella said while leaning in to look at the waitress's name tag, "Toobah, right?" The waitress sighed again but nodded. "How would you like to earn an additional ten percent on our check?"

"What are you talking about?"

DeKella winked at Harr. "If you treat us with respect, act helpfully, and bring our food promptly, yet properly prepared, I'll give you ten percent, in credits, of whatever our final bill is tonight."

"So, wait," Toobah said dubiously, "you're telling me that if I pretend to give a crap about you and your weird pal here, and your bill turns out to be one hundred credits, you'll give ten additional credits directly to me?"

"That's what I'm saying," agreed DeKella.

The waitress said, "Huh," in a thoughtful way. Then, she took a moment to compose herself. She removed the wad of gum from her mouth and launched it expertly into the trash bin that sat near the far wall. She then smoothed out her pants and shirt, and ran her fingers through her hair.

Finally, she turned back and began speaking in a professional turnaround from how she'd spoken just moments before. "Many people request the *Gurgling Shark* to be cooked medium-rare, sir. Honestly, though, I would recommend against that dish tonight as it is not exactly fresh."

"Oh?" said Harr, sitting up a little taller. "What would you suggest?"

"The *Fiery Wortbird* is most excellent. It comes with a side of fried *Bloodsnakes* that have been known to win awards on occasion."

"Great. I'll have that."

"Excellent," she said with what Harr considered to be a genuine smile. "And you, ma'am?"

"*Flowering Sazobird* with a side of fried *Xeno*."

"Brilliant selection, ma'am," Toobah said with a bow,

taking the menus from the table. "I'll put in your order and will have your dinner out shortly."

DeKella's mouth was hanging open in utter shock as Toobah walked away. Harr gave her a conspiratorial shrug as he sipped his wine. It was quite delicious. Full bodied with a hint of sweet, but it had a nice dry edge to it as well.

"I can't believe that just happened," she said. "That was simply amazing."

"It's funny how quickly money can change a person's perspective."

"I'll have to tell all my friends about this."

"Or," Harr suggested, setting his glass down and putting his elbows on the table, "you could keep it a secret. That way your friends will be shocked at how well you're treated whenever you go out. Prestige, you know?"

"Yet another *fabulous* idea," DeKella said with a look of awe. "You're just full of them."

"I'm definitely full of something," Harr somewhat agreed.

FURTHER INTEL

*G*eneral Struggins had just put the finishing touches on a perfect putt from the edge of the green. He was only able to get out to the course once a week ever since the warp technology had moved from theory to potentiality. If everything went to plan, though, he'd put the sticks up in trade for a seat on the command chair of the finest space-faring war vessel ever imagined. Distant worlds would fold under the fierceness of the Kallian military. Once he'd built it, of course.

He was sliding the putter back into the bag when he saw Private Deddles approaching. Perfect timing.

"Ah, Deddles," he said as he motioned toward the bag, "carry that for me."

"Yes, sir."

They headed toward the main clubhouse. A nice cheese sandwich and a beer or two always hit the spot after 18 holes.

"I'm assuming you've been out of my sight because you were doing something that needs to be done, yes?"

"I was, sir."

"And what, pray tell, was it that you did?"

"I got information on the inspectors, sir," Deddles said proudly.

"Did you now?" Struggins did his best to look and sound surprised. "Well, that's mighty industrious of you, son. Although, I would be remiss if I didn't chastise you for such an action. You are aware that it is clearly against regulations to have garnered intel on the inspectors, I hope?"

"Yes, sir," Deddles said with grin and a wink.

Struggins decided to ignore that. "And yet you—and do note that I'm clearly stating that *you* did this, Deddles—decided to run on out and gather data on the inspection crew of your own volition?"

"I did what needed to be done, sir."

Struggins actually stopped at this point and gave Deddles an appraising glance. The boy was about as sharp as a golf ball but it was marginally possible that he was more than just a gun jockey. Struggins harrumphed with surprise and resumed his walk.

"Well, Deddles, I'll have to reprimand you for this transgression, obviously, but since the deed has already been done I suppose it can't hurt to know what you've learned."

"Reprimanded, sir?"

"Has to be done, Deddles," Struggins said seriously. "The military can't allow regulations to be broken without some form of consequence. It just wouldn't be militarily sound."

"Oh."

"Again, though, since there's no way to un-flush a toilet, as it were, I'd like to understand what you gleaned in your research."

"Yes, sir," Deddles said, placing the bag alongside of the other bags that sat in the rack by the clubhouse entrance. He pulled out a sheet of paper and slowly unfolded it. Then he spun it around. "The main inspector, sir, is a Dr. Zep Welder.

His assistants are Drs. Fleeka Baloo, Grayle Piffer, and Dangly N. Impotent."

"Go on," Struggins said.

"They're staying at the 3 Seasons Hotel across from Good Times Leeko's."

"Right by the W.A.R.P.E.D. building. Yes, I know where those places are. What else?"

"Uh…" Deddles flipped the paper over a couple of times, obviously searching for something else to add. "Ah, yes! Dr. Impotent has a short tail, sir."

Struggins lowered himself onto the bench and rubbed his chin firmly.

"Deddles," he said coolly, "are you telling me that you only got their names?"

"No, sir," Deddles answered. "I also know where they're staying. Floor and everything."

"I see." Struggins sighed and began to take in the view of the golf course. The sun was descending down toward the horizon. It still had a couple of hours to go being that it was summer, but he tried his best to return to the clubhouse at this time of the day because the view soothed him. "Deddles," he said, "can you give me an idea of how I can use the information that you've just given me? I could have just as easily walked up to the guard at the front desk of the W.A.R.P.E.D. building and asked him for that intel."

"That's what I did, sir," Deddles said as if surprised.

"You disappoint me, Private. Here I was thinking that you'd gone and found a way to make yourself useful to that uniform that you're wearing. Instead, you mark yourself as a complete waste of carbon, yet again." He shook his head, no longer finding himself interested in ordering a sandwich. "Now, unless you have something more to report, I'd suggest you go and start cleaning all of the latrines on barracks 119 as part of your punishment for attempting—

albeit poorly—to spy in on the records of our esteemed inspection crew."

"Yes, sir," Deddles said with a slouch. He turned and started to walk away but then stopped. "Oh, there is one more thing, sir."

"Shoe sizes?"

"No, sir."

"Favorite brand of toothpaste, maybe?"

"I didn't think that would help, sir. Would it?"

"Just tell me what it is, Deddles."

Deddles squared himself. "Right before I arrived at the golf course, sir, I heard a news report that the airplane carrying the inspectors never arrived at the airport."

"What?" Struggins said, bolting up from the bench.

"Yes, sir. The plane left on Northsouth Airlines, flight number NS112, from Akember Bay. But that flight hasn't landed yet."

"Is there some reason that you didn't lead with that information, Private Deddles?"

"I didn't think it was important, sir. I mean, the inspectors are already here, right?"

Struggins looked back across the golf course with a grin.

"Maybe not."

PLACING BOMBS

"*T*hat's one whacked-out broad," said Geezer while watching the video feed that came in from Vool's eyes.

"She's a soldier," Sandoo replied, as if that made everything okay. "Any good soldier knows that following orders without question is what needs to be done."

"Are you nuts?" Geezer said. He put down the wrench he'd been holding and picked up his workman's towel and began wiping his hands clean. He knew he didn't need to wipe his hands, but it was in his makeup to do it. "Following orders without question is stupidity. I mean, sure, if they make sense that's fine, but if they're insane," —he tilted his head toward the screen that Vool was on as a case-in-point— "then you kind of need to stand up and say something."

Sandoo shifted uneasily. "No offense, Geezer, but you're not a soldier so you can't possibly understand."

Well, that was a bit offensive, if not a little hurtful. Hadn't Geezer just gone through the same boot camp that Sandoo had? No, he hadn't done all the push-ups and such that they had done, but they didn't have to drag their batteries around on a tray like he did, either.

"I went through boot camp on Sadian just like everyone else."

"True," Sandoo answered with a nod, "but that's not really the same thing."

"Don't belittle my service, pal." Geezer tucked the towel back into the pocket on his hip. "Just because I haven't seen any action since going through boot camp doesn't mean that I should be treated like anything less than what I've trained for. Hell, boy, before you were even a mishmash of those initial zeroes and ones that your programmers rigged up, I was out in ships like the *Reluctant,* here, getting my feet wet in engineering. And I can tell you that I've been in far more encounters than you have."

The air grew silent as the two resumed their stares at the image of Vool walking around in the lab of the W.A.R.P.E.D. building. It was a creepy thing watching the world through someone else's eyes. While they had no way of knowing what was going through her mind, the angle of her head and the squinting of her eyelids made Geezer feel like she saw the world in a very angry way.

"I'm sorry, sir," Sandoo said after a time. "I didn't meant to imply…"

"I know what you meant, dude," Geezer said icily, "and as your superior officer, I would have to say…"

"I'm sorry, what?"

"What what?"

"Did you just claim to be my superior officer?"

Geezer turned to face Sandoo. "Everyone knows that a ship's engineer outranks every member of the ship except for the captain."

"I'm sorry to inform you that you are incorrect, sir," Sandoo replied.

"Who is higher ranked than me?"

"Well," Sandoo said, "me, for one."

"You? But you always call me 'sir.'"

"I call everyone that, except for the ladies, of course. It's just, as you put it, in my mishmash of zeroes and ones."

This was unsettling news, to be sure. Geezer had always assumed that, besides the captain, he was the most important member of the ship. Who else could have hooked them up with all the gadgetry that he'd managed over the years?

"So who else is higher ranked than me?"

"Lieutenant Moon and Lieutenant Ridly."

"Seriously?"

"Also Ensigns Middleton and Curr."

"Holy crap. You can't be serious."

"Sorry."

"Please tell me that I'm not beneath Jezden," Geezer begged, recognizing how wrong that sounded but taking comfort in the fact that Sandoo's mind was never in the gutter.

"No, you're above him," Sandoo said. "Middleton and Curr are second-level ensigns. Jezden is still first, and will likely always be."

"Oh," Geezer said with a relieved laugh. "Well, that's a relief."

"You're ranked the same."

His head sprang up. "What?"

"Before you get too upset," Sandoo said calmly, "that's only if you decided to go the route of soldier; otherwise, you're probably the most important person on this ship... including the captain."

"You think?" he asked. His confidence was in serious need of a boost.

"I do," Sandoo said. "At least the most important robot, anyway."

"Hey…I'm the *only* robot."

"See?"

"Right."

"Anyway," Sandoo said quickly, pointing at the screen, "we should get back to tracking Vool. What is she up to?"

They watched as Vool walked around the lab. She was clearly waiting for some privacy as she kept ducking behind machinery every time someone got close. Finally, she moved to the middle of the room and glanced all around, demonstrating that she was most assuredly up to no good.

She reached down and pulled out a small device from her coat pocket, played with the wires on the back of it, and then reached under one of the handrails near the big chamber and pressed it into place.

After another quick scan around the room, she repeated this on the other side of the chamber.

"What's she doing?" asked Sandoo.

"She's placing explosives," Geezer answered while keeping his eyes focused on looking out at the world through Vool's eyes.

"So the captain was right," Sandoo said with a hiss. "She *is* up to something."

"Looks that way."

"We should report…"

A ringing sound interrupted the commander.

Geezer looked around to see where it might be coming from. It wasn't familiar. At first he thought it may be originating through Vool, but then he remembered that they hadn't put any auditory devices on her.

It rang again.

"What the hell is that?" Geezer said as he fished around on his desk. Finally, the thing revealed itself sitting on the shelf beside him. It was shaped like a brick and colored like one, too. The difference was that this thing had lights on it and it was heavier than a brick. He pressed the only glowing button and said, "Hello?"

"Hello?" came a voice from the device. "Hello? Can y... hear m...?"

"Uh, sort of," Geezer replied. "You're kind of breaking up."

"Sec...okay, can you hear me now?"

"Yeah, that's better."

"Good. Sometimes it's hard to get a signal. You know how these intergalactic relays can be."

"Not really, no," said Geezer. "Who is this, again?"

"It's your boss."

"Uh, you don't sound like Captain Harr," Geezer said while Sandoo was mouthing, "Who is it?" Geezer just shrugged.

"Sorry. I'm *his* boss."

"Frexle?" Geezer ventured.

"Correct, and who is this?"

"Geezer, and I'm here with Commander Sandoo."

"Put me on speaker," Frexle stated.

"How?"

"Just set the phone down."

Geezer did and then heard a click.

"Uh...hello?" Geezer said, but got nothing in return.

"I think you disconnected the call," Sandoo pointed out. "That's probably not a good thing to do to your boss."

It rang again. "Hello?"

"Put it down on its back," Frexle said. "If you put it face down that will hang up on me. These minutes aren't cheap, you know."

"Right, sorry." Geezer set the phone down. "You still there?"

"Yes. Can you both hear me okay?"

"Yep," answered Geezer.

"Yes, sir," said Sandoo.

"Good. Now, listen. I shouldn't be contacting you, but I fear that Vool is planning to sabotage that test tomorrow. She's likely going to be placing explosives somewhere, though I couldn't tell you where."

"My guess would be in the lab where they're doing tests," said Geezer as he watched Vool doing that very thing.

"Probably."

"No 'probably' about it, boss-man," Geezer said. "She's already placed three of the buggers in there."

"You have to stop her."

"We're on it, sir," confirmed Sandoo. "Captain Harr did not trust Vool from the get-go, so he had us put view-film on her contact lenses and a tracking device in her tail."

"I'm sorry," Frexle said sounding like a man who was baffled, "did you say in her tail?"

"Yes, sir."

"How the hell did you get her to agree to that? Maybe that Jezden fellow…"

"They're wearing disguises to blend in with the Kallians, chief," said Geezer. "The Kallians have tails. It's prosthetic."

"Ah, I see. Well, here is some information you don't know. She's planning to press the button on those explosives at the same time the Kallians start their test."

"We'll have those bombs disconnected before then, sir," Sandoo said smartly.

"How?"

"How, sir?"

"Yes, how?" Frexle said. "These aren't some run-of-the mill explosives you're looking at here, Commander. They can't just be turned off with a flick of a switch."

"Oh."

"What's the tech?" asked Geezer. "Some kind of DNA matrix?"

"No, nothing like that."

"Proximity switch, then?"

"Actually, no," Frexle replied, "but that's an interesting idea."

"Made one a long time back," said Geezer, "when the Segnal Space Marine Corps decided to shut down the G.3.3.Z.3.R. line. Wanted to cover my ass."

"You'll have to tell me more about that sometime," Frexle said. "These devices are like nothing you've ever seen. There are two chemical chambers that are connected with a tube. In that tube is a piece of metal that keeps the solutions separated. A little explosive device is connected to a set of three wires. It's triggered from a remote by entering in the proper numerical sequence and then pressing the 'boom' button."

"Boom button," Sandoo confirmed.

"You said three wires, honcho?"

"Correct," Frexle answered. "Red, yellow, and green. You have to cut one."

"I can't cut one, hot dog. I'm a robot. Remember?"

"Sorry, what?"

"Bad joke," Geezer said apologetically. "You were saying?"

"One of the wires has to be cut. If you choose the wrong one, end of story. The mixture of that chemical composition will take out the entire planet."

"Those little devices are that powerful?" Sandoo said with wide eyes.

"A single one of them will do the job, Commander. Vool is just being extra certain."

"So you just cut the red wire, then," Geezer stated. "That should do it."

"Now, listen carefully," began Frexle. Then he stopped. "Wait, how did you know that?"

"Honestly," Geezer said while leaning back in his chair,

"you guys have *never* seen *Stellar Hike*? I'm finding that really hard to believe. Or, maybe you've seen *McKorkler?*"

"Neither of them," admitted Frexle.

"Not even the *Z Team?*"

"Sorry, I've never heard of it."

"Amazing show," said Geezer. "I especially liked the guy with the ear-to-ear Mohawk. He started a craze with that thing. He was one funny cat."

"I'm not following you," Frexle said after a few seconds.

"It's simple, boss. You've got three wires, just like in all those shows. If you cut the red wire, it shuts off the bomb. Cut the yellow and it sets up a thirty-minute countdown. Clip the green one, though, and you've got an instant *kapow.*"

"Precisely," Frexle said, sounding astonished.

"Nothing to it, boss. It's all on TV."

"I've clearly got to seek out new shows from new civilizations," Frexle said. "It's frowned upon here in Overseer-land, but I'm going to boldly watch what no Overseer has watched before."

"Oh, come on," Geezer bellowed in his robotic way. "That's basically the tag line for *Stellar Hike!*"

"Honestly? That's amazing. Well, anyway, it sounds as if you *do* know how to deactivate the bombs."

"We'll have it resolved tonight, sir," Sandoo said as Geezer just sat shaking his head in disbelief.

"Great. I've got to say that you people are kind of impressing me."

"Thank you, sir."

"Frexle, out."

Geezer sat staring at the brick-shaped device. The lights were still glowing. He wondered how the thing had gotten onto the ship, and specifically how it arrived in his office. He assumed that Frexle had transported it in before the *Reluctant* departed the station. These Overseers were simultaneously powerful and stupid, from Geezer's perspective.

"That was nice of him to call," Sandoo said.

"Something in it for him, no doubt," replied Geezer. "That's the way it is with dumbass bosses."

"I'm still on the line," Frexle said.

"Oh, sorry," Geezer said as his head drooped. He flipped over the phone. "Well, that'll teach me a lesson."

"What do you mean?" Sandoo asked.

"Just that I've got to be one hundred percent certain that a stupid boss isn't within earshot when calling him a dumbass."

"Still here."

"Damn it," Geezer said, picking up the brick. "How the hell do you disconnect this piece of crap? I thought you said to just put it on the other side?"

"There are four sides," answered Frexle. "Put it down on the side that says 'hang up,' dumbass."

"Right."

SPYING

*S*ince it was getting late, most of the personnel had left for the evening. The command room still had a number of monitors flipped on and the sound of whirring fans in the vast set of computers offered a general hum of white noise that could drown out mental chatter.

General Struggins understood that he needed soldiers, but there was something about working with just a small team that made him feel like things were actually getting done, even if one of those soldiers was Private Deddles. The other, Technician Ewups, one of those individuals who Struggins' grandkids referred to as a "geek" was so close to his computer screen that he wondered how the boy remained pale. Not due to radiation, just simply from the brightness of the light smacking the kid in the face. From the look of Ewups, Struggins assumed that he wouldn't last more than two minutes in actual sunshine. The boy was also pudgy. This was expected in the Technician side of the military, but Struggins had never liked it. If Ewups had gone through standard boot camp like Deddles had, though, he would have been washed out before the end of the first day. Then again, Deddles wouldn't last an hour in the version of boot camp that Ewups had gone through. Struggins would be surprised if Deddles could even turn a damn computer on, much less use it for anything helpful.

"We need to put an eye on that Dr. Welder," said Struggins, "or whatever his name actually is."

"What about his assistants, sir?" asked Deddles.

Struggins didn't mind the occasional suggestion from a soldier, but Deddles had a tendency of grating on the nerves, so when he suggested something, it rubbed Struggins the wrong way.

"Look around this room, Private," he said sternly. "Who would you say is running the show here?"

"You are, sir," Deddles said after a quick look around.

"And what happens when I don't run the show, Private?"

"Things get fouled up, sir?"

"Things get fouled up," Struggins affirmed. "What does that tell you, Deddles?"

"I don't know, sir."

"It tells you that whoever is in charge is the one who makes the decisions."

"Yes, sir."

"Now, let's say that you wanted to have someone keep tabs on our group, Deddles," Struggins said, and then quickly added, "hypothetically speaking, of course." He didn't want Deddles to get into his head that there was a desire from his commanding officer to have his personal crew under surveillance. Mostly because they already were and he didn't want Deddles, or anyone else for that matter, to find out about it. He didn't do it to glean information, as that would be pointless. He kept an eye on them to make sure they were doing as they were told. "Would you bother keepings tabs on the likes of yourself?"

"Yes, sir."

"No, you wouldn't, Deddles," Struggins patiently corrected the private. "The reason you wouldn't is because you're not a decision-maker. I am. So you would keep your eyes on me. To do otherwise would be an utter waste of time and resources. Do you understand that, Private?"

"I do, sir. Thank you, sir."

"Good. Just to make sure we're clear on this, can you tell me why we shouldn't bother keeping tabs on those who don't make the decisions?"

"Because the people who aren't the decision-makers, sir, do not need to be followed because they are being told what to do by those who *are* the decision-makers, sir."

"Not bad, Deddles," Struggins said with surprise. "Not bad at all. To drive the point home, though, I'll add that good leaders never let subordinates do anything too important. So, seeing that we have no interest in watching Dr. Welder's assistants fill out forms, flip switches, or whatever it is that inspectors do, I'd say that we should just keep our eyes on Welder alone."

"Understood, sir."

It probably wasn't understood, but as long as Deddles did as he was told, which he most often did because he wasn't exactly what you'd call a "self-starter," things would go smoothly enough. With any luck, Ewups would prove more beneficial to their current cause.

"Ewups, are we connected to the video network yet?"

"Yes, sir," Ewups said in a voice that cracked now and again. "Dr. Welder and Dr. DeKella have just exited Good Time Leeko's."

"That place has a great *Snarling Bloodstick* appetizer," Struggins said absently. His stomach was growling since he hadn't gone in for the sandwich at the clubhouse earlier.

"I like their *Vulcanic Hawk*," Deddles said.

"I'm more of a *Swaying Drunk Turnip Roast* kind of guy, myself," Ewups added.

Damn hippies.

"Deddles," Struggins said as his hunger won him over, "remember how I was saying that leaders do the important stuff and delegate the lesser items to their underlings?"

"Yes, sir."

"Go pick up some food for us," he commanded. "Ewups and I will watch the feeds."

"Yes, sir," Deddles said glumly.

Struggins had recovered a bit from his irritation at the boy's lack of intelligence-gathering prowess, but he still couldn't help but sit amazed at how the military had changed since the time he'd enlisted. It used to be that soldiering was what young people got into because they felt a sense of pride in serving Kallian.

Wars were a thing of the past, except the occasional skirmish between start-up groups and terrorists, but even those were few and far between. After the last major war, the various countries had pulled together to create a single governing body, which meant it had a single military. Struggins was near the top of that militaristic chain of command, though not so far up that he'd become moot. He was a 13-Star General, and that meant he still had time to make a difference. The day a general was awarded his 16th star was the day that things went downhill. Being a 20-Star General—the highest rank on Kallian—meant that you essentially became a figurehead. You went to parties, waved at people, and shook the hands of cadets. Day-to-day operations fell back on those at the 15-Star General level and below. Plus, in order to hit 20-Stars, you'd have to be damn near 100 years old anyway, which typically meant adult diapers, incessant drooling, and not even knowing where you were half the time.

Regardless, he hated the thought processes of today's recruits, but their numbers were dwindling and so the Kallian military had to take what they could get. It was a volunteer service, unlike in his day when a minimum of four years was mandatory for any able-bodied Kallian. Last checked, the volunteer numbers were a dismal 4.7 percent. Just a decade ago, they were in the mid-twenties. Those who did volunteer typically had an angle, such as having their debt wiped out, or getting money for education, or learning a new skill, or all three. The Debt-Wiper Bill was probably the most ambitious tool for adding recruits, but it didn't perform quite as expected because the military didn't accept volunteers over the age of 25. Most people didn't get to a scary level of debt until hitting 40.

What Struggins hoped for was that one day he'd have a space fleet in place where intelligent, strong young people came out of the woodwork begging to join up so that they could travel to the stars.

"Waste of a good soldier's uniform," Struggins said under his breath as Deddles shut the door.

"Sir?"

"Nothing, Ewups." Struggins pointed toward the geek's screen. "Just keep an eye on that video. Where are they now?"

"They seem to be heading to Dr. DeKella's apartment."

"Please tell me we have her place bugged?" Struggins said hopefully.

"Yes, sir. I installed it myself last year when you implied that I could improve my station from Technician to Sr. Technician if I only learned to do what needed to be done, sir."

"Yes, yes," Struggins said with a wince. "I remember that. I finally got your paperwork on my desk just a couple of weeks back, as a matter of fact." Whether that was true or not, Struggins truly had no idea. "Haven't had a chance to look them over just yet, but if you do well in this little spy game of ours, I assure you that my pen will be in-hand before the weekend."

The proverbial carrot had been placed. Struggins hated it, but that's the way it was with today's soldiers. The satisfaction of doing one's duty had been replaced with the "What's in it for me?" mentality.

"Yes, sir," Ewups said, sitting straight up and refocusing. "Thank you, sir."

HER PLACE

$\mathcal{D}$r. DeKella's apartment was nicer than even the hotel that Harr and his crew had been hooked up with. The furniture was contemporary by his standards. Sleek lines and bright patterns were the theme. He was used to high ceilings being the norm for most places on Segnal, but they were low compared to DeKella's place. She was on a top floor, though, which may have garnered her that extra ceiling height. All of Harr's past dwellings were typically on ground level.

"Nice place you have here," he said as she sat across from him on the couch, after first handing him a glass of wine.

"I wish I could take credit," DeKella replied. "It came furnished."

"Well, I suppose you had to have selected which one to rent in the first place, so you can still take some credit."

"That's true," she said with a laugh. "Well, not really. It was one of my interns who found it for me."

"Oh." Harr took a pull on the wine. "Still, it's nice."

"I had wanted a place in the suburbs, but with all of the work going on, it just seemed more fitting to be close by.

Frankly, I would have preferred something a little less ostentatious. I'm a simple girl who likes simple things."

"Same here."

"You're a simple girl who likes simple things?" DeKella cracked a smile.

"Funny," Harr said, raising his glass. "If this scientist thing doesn't work out, you might consider comedy."

His mind was racing, though he tried to maintain a calm demeanor. It had been a while since he'd been this interested in a member of the opposite sex. It was obviously poor timing, but such was the way of things for an intergalactic traveler. At least that's what he was trying to convince himself of.

The fact was that he was falling for this woman. Ridly and Vool knew it, and Jezden could have spied it a mile away, but Harr understood that there could be no relationship here. She was a Kallian and he was a—well, past-Segnalian. He guessed they could have a long-distance relationship, measured in light years, but that wouldn't be fair to her. Besides, what if he happened upon another mission and fell for another woman? Harr wasn't the cheating type. The reality, though, at least if you followed the trend of shows like *Stellar Hike*, was that Harr was a space-ship captain and that meant he was bound to garner the attention of many hot alien chicks.

"I know you can't give me the details of where you're from, Zep," DeKella said, "but I find you and your team to be quite different than most people."

"Inspectors are an odd lot, I suppose."

"No argument there, but that's not what I'm talking about. I've worked with inspectors from all over the world and they all share in some basic similarities. They all know that there are male and female sides to a menu, for example. They also know that gentlemen order first at a restaurant. And none of them have ever heard of tipping a waiter."

"Obviously," he said carefully, "you've not met anyone from my particular part of the world."

"Is there no television in your particular part of the world?" she said challengingly. "Seems you'd pick up the basics of things just from watching a show or two in your lifetime."

Damn. If she kept up with this line of questioning, she'd eventually figure something out. There wasn't much chance she was going to jump to the conclusion that he was from another world, but Harr had to think quickly.

"Once the test is a success," he said, knowing that this would never happen, "maybe I'll take you for a trip to my homeland. Then all of your questions will be answered."

"Promise?"

Harr shrugged noncommittally. He couldn't make that promise. First off, where exactly would he take her? Segnal was out of the question. He couldn't risk being seen there after everything that had happened. Not that his face was on a Most Wanted poster or anything, but who was to say what'd happened since he'd left home? Bringing her to Overseer-land was an even more ridiculous idea. It wasn't his home anyway. The only place that really was "home" to him and his band of androids was the *Reluctant*. Not exactly a homeland, per se, but it's all he had to offer.

She smiled and slowly pulled the band out of her hair, letting it fall in long waves down the sides of her face. She'd had that reserved librarian thing going all day, but now she was a woman full of desire. Harr gulped.

"What say we quit with the small talk, doctor?"

It had been a long time since he'd gone beyond small talk. At least with someone else. Of course he never bothered with the small talk when he was alone. "Yeah, okay. I mean, sure.

Right." He set his wine glass down. "Do you mind if I use your restroom first?"

DeKella gave him a very odd look indeed. "Of course," she said as though catching herself. She then pointed toward the main hallway. "It's right through there. Second door on the right."

"I'll just be a moment."

"I'll be waiting."

CUTTING THE WIRES

*R*idly and Jezden entered the lab with clippers in-hand. Geezer had provided them with the details on where Vool had placed the charges, and now it was up to them to cut the red wires and be done with it.

There were still a few scientists working, but they were so engrossed in what they were doing that they paid little mind to the inspectors. Ridly assumed that they were more worried that they'd be questioned if they said anything. All in all, she couldn't blame them. Even as an android, she had no desire to be held up to scrutiny.

"Okay," she said as they approached the Multicombo Chamber, "Geezer said that they're on stations one, seven, and thirteen. This should be a snap. Small wires aren't much of a challenge."

"Was that yet another insult attempt regarding the size of my tail, Ridly?" Jezden said with a groan.

"What?" she replied, looking confused. Then she slowly broke into a grin. "Oh, you mean because your tail is of the nearly record-breaking variety? I hadn't even considered the comparison," she said, placing her hand on his arm. "Mostly because I think the wires may be more impressive."

Jezden gaped at her and yanked his arm away. "I don't think you understand how this is affecting me."

Ridly knelt down and found the first explosive. It was small indeed, but she could clearly make out the three wires that Geezer had mentioned. She carefully reached in and snipped the red one, and then pulled the two ends to opposite sides so that they wouldn't accidentally touch again.

"Serves you right," she said while walking to the next section. "You never seem to care about how your comments affect others. Not much fun being on the receiving end, is it?" She reached down to look for the second explosive, but stopped and said, "Then again, you've been on the receiving end before, right? On Merrymoon, if memory serves."

The women on the Merrymoon mission had taken a shine to Jezden, which was a common theme wherever he went...until Kallian. Seeing that the men on Merrymoon weren't all that attractive, yet the women were incredibly so, Jezden thought he'd died and gone to android nirvana. But things didn't quite turn out the way he'd expected.

"Hey now," Jezden warned, "the captain made us promise to never bring that up. What happens on Merrymoon stays on Merrymoon. We were just out looking for the *SSMC Voyeur,* and that's it. That's all we're supposed to say on that subject."

"Captain's not here," she said teasingly. "What are you going to do, tell?"

"Just finish up the damn job."

They moved toward station thirteen when one of the scientists came up to them. She was taller than most Kallians and possessed a tail that demonstrated a hefty dose of virility. Beyond that, she had what Ridly could only describe as swagger.

"I'm Dr. Levton," she said to Jezden specifically, "and I'd like to speak with you."

"Sure," he said after giving Ridly a wry smile. She rolled her eyes in response. "What can I help you with?"

"You've got an incredibly small tail," she said, looking him over.

Ridly snickered.

"Here we go," Jezden said with a groan.

"Does anyone…" Levton paused and focused on Ridly. "Actually, I apologize. Are you two a couple?"

"No," Ridly said quickly. "We just work together. Please, pretend I'm not even here."

"It'd be better if you actually *weren't* here," Jezden said out of the corner of his mouth.

"I should have asked that first," Levton said to Ridly. "When I see a small tail, my brain changes levels."

"Completely understandable," Ridly replied. "They are such a turn-off, aren't they?"

"On the contrary," Levton replied with her eyebrows up. "I find them quite interesting."

"Really?" said Jezden and Ridly in unison.

"Everyone knows that people with small tails are submissive-minded," Levton said.

"What?" Jezden said with a start.

"Hush, you," Levton said to Jezden in a stern voice. "The long tails are speaking."

"Yes, Dr. Impotent," Ridly said with a chuckle, "you should know better."

Jezden closed his eyes and shook his head. Ridly was already having a blast making fun of how his ego-driven choice to have a small tail had backfired, but this just put things over the top.

"Anyway," Levton continued, "if he doesn't belong to you,

I was going to see if he was looking for someone to belong to."

"I don't belong to any..."

"Oh no," Ridly interrupted as if he weren't even in the room, "I've known him a long time. He doesn't belong to anyone. But I'd wager he'd like to."

"What?" Jezden said. "Let me tell you something..."

Dr. Levton put her hands on her hips. "You're obviously in need of training," she said.

"I'll have you know..."

"Can it, small tail," Ridly said as seriously as she could muster, but she was dying from laughter on the inside.

"Seriously?" Jezden said to Ridly. Then he turned back to Levton. "What is it with you people and small tails, anyway? What's the big deal?"

"Besides the fact that you're all submissive?"

"I'm not submissive," Jezden replied.

"Merrymoon," Ridly pointed out.

"They were giants, Ridly," Jezden said. "It wasn't like I had much of a choice. And we're not supposed to talk about that!"

"It's Dr. Baloo, thank you very much," Ridly replied.

"Look, lady," Jezden said, turning to look at Dr. Levton, "I don't know what it is that makes you think that just because I have a small tail that I'm submissive, but I'm not. And frankly, I resent the stereotype."

"Hmmm," Levton said after a moment. "This is interesting."

"What is?"

"I think I find you even more attractive now that you're talking to me this way."

"Well," Jezden said while flashing his pearly whites, "most women can't resist me."

"No, that's not it. I guess I just like a bit of a challenge."

Jezden crossed his arms and turned very serious. "Go away, lady."

"Interesting," she said as she spun on her heel and sensually walked away.

"You know…"

"Shut up, Ridly," Jezden said. "I'm not in the mood."

"That's a first," Ridly replied as she knelt back down to take care of the wires. "Must come with the territory of being Dr. Impotent."

SPYING AGAIN

General Struggins had just cleaned his fingers after devouring his order of *Snarling Bloodstick* when he noticed that a couple of inspectors had come back to the lab. He assumed that they were just taking advantage of the quieter atmosphere due to the late hour. Wise, if that were the case. He much preferred the late hour when getting things done was a priority.

They were two of the junior inspectors, too, so the likelihood of finding any interest in what they were doing was low. As he'd said before, underlings were always given the unimportant tasks.

Still, there was something about the way they were moving that gave him pause. He couldn't help but feel that mischief was on their agenda.

"Deddles," he said, pointing down toward the lab, "do those two look suspicious to you?"

"Those are the inspectors, sir."

"I'm aware of who they are, Private. I'm more worried about what it is they're doing."

"My guess is that they're inspecting things, sir."

"I mean specifically, you moron."

"Uh…"

"Goodness, boy," Struggins said while furrowing his brow, "show some initiative. I don't know how many times I have to say it before you get it through your skull. And me *telling* you all the time to do something is not the same thing. You have to do things on your own."

"Yes, sir."

He waited, but Deddles just remained standing there. Bottom line was that if Struggins ever died, this place would fall apart, unless another like him came in to take over.

"Deddles, get on one of those infernal machines and train a camera on them," he commanded in a not-so-nice way. "Figure out what the hell they're doing." Then he turned to the technician and said, "Ewups, what's the status on Welder and DeKella?"

"Last I heard, things were starting to get hot and heavy," Ewups answered, "but then Dr. Welder said he had to use the bathroom."

"That's disturbing," Struggins said with a look of distaste.

"Yeah," Ewups agreed.

These inspectors were getting odder by the moment. They had an air about them that felt wrong. That wasn't a stereotype, either. These inspectors didn't quite fit any particular stereotype that Struggins could think of.

"Sir," Deddles said from the other terminal, "it looks like they're clipping wires on some device."

"Let me see that." Struggins pushed Deddles out of the way and plopped down into the chair. He zoomed in the camera and his eyes bulged. "That's a bomb, private."

"A real one, sir?"

"Of course it's a real one, you nincompoop!" Honestly, what kind of weeding out process did the military use these days? He shook his head and refocused on the feed. "Looks like they're activating it. Everyone knows that when you cut the red wire it starts the countdown."

"Just like on *Moon Adventure*," Ewups said.

"What do we do, sir?"

"Simple, Deddles. As soon as they leave, we go back in and hook those damn wires right back up."

"That makes sense, sir," Deddles said, looking relieved. "Great thinking, sir."

"Gotta be on your toes to be a general, boy," Struggins stated firmly. "Start using that noggin of yours and maybe, though doubtfully, you'll make it to lieutenant one day."

"Thank you, sir." Deddles was beaming for a moment, but then frowned. "Why not general, sir?"

"Just trying to be realistic," Struggins said, wishing he'd had another order of *Snarling Bloodstick*. "Bending the realism enough already with the concept of you making it to lieutenant, Deddles."

THE RIDGWAY CONVERTER

*N*o matter what he did, Geezer couldn't figure out what the hell was holding up the transporter from working correctly. The physics were stupid, of course, but that'd never stopped him from accomplishing things before.

After much study, he finally found something that could pull it all together. It was called the *Ridgway Converter*, though some scientists referred to it as the *Jelboobah's Witness Converter*.

It was an ingenious device that had the sole purpose of making other pieces of technology believe that there was a higher technological power that wanted them to do their jobs without rational thought, even if those jobs were improbable, impossible, or nonsensical.

The device was named after Dr. David Ridgway, a scientist from Segnal who stumbled upon the idea for the converter when two Jelboobah's Witnesses showed up at his door one day. He had tried to push them along their merry way, but they simply wouldn't take "no" for an answer. They were so adept at their conversion abilities, that they had Dr.

Ridgway seriously considering whether or not there truly was a hell. After about 15 minutes, he felt that he was actually *in* hell. Finally, he took the pamphlet with a terrified smile and promised that he'd put serious thought to their points of view. Once they had left, Dr. Ridgway's brain reengaged and he promptly launched the pamphlet into the flame canister with a shake of his head. When he returned to his work, though, he began to wonder if he couldn't somehow use the same tactics to guilt pieces of technology into reacting in certain ways. He immediately set upon working on a device that could convert other devices into *its* way of thinking. The underlying theme was that if the tech didn't succumb, it would suffer an eternity on the scrap heap. The good doctor was more surprised than anyone that the device had actually worked. It even landed him a *Slobel Prize* in two fields: technology and religion. Unfortunately, Jelboobah's Witness engineers got their hands on the device and twisted it in such a way that it had convinced all of the vending machines on Segnal that they should become Jelboobah's Witnesses. Not long after this, Dr. Ridgway was expelled from normal society, forced to live out his days as a nomad, dodging launched tomatoes and kicks in his pants each time he visited town. Rightfully so, too, as it's rather aggravating having to sit through a sermon every time you wanted a carbonated beverage. No, it wasn't directly his fault that this happened, any more than it's the gun-maker's fault that someone invented bullets, but repercussions tend to flow much like shit and every invention had to have a face to put to any failures. It wasn't like they were going to try and expel the Jelboobah's Witnesses. That would have caused all sorts of religious uprisings, discussions, and conversions. Throwing tomatoes at them and kicking them in the pants was fine, and quite commonplace, but ousting Dr. Ridgway was a far simpler option.

Geezer set to work putting up firewalls and security measures to make sure that the *Reluctant* didn't get infiltrated. He was adamantly opposed to having to tell Captain Harr that the ship was now a member of the religiosity. This was barely possible since there weren't any Jelboobah's Witnesses on board—at least not that Geezer was aware of. It would take someone with extraordinary skill, or in Geezer's case, luck, to make the tech work anyway.

And if he could get this thing functioning as he'd hoped, it might help him locate and *convert* Frexle's tracking device.

Three hours into the integration, Sandoo stepped into the room. "Have you heard back from Ridly and Jezden?"

"No, but I've not really been paying much attention." He spun to the datapad and saw a message from Ridly. "They clipped the wires. We're all good."

"Great," Sandoo said, but he didn't leave. Instead, he was just sort of milling around.

"Something else?"

"No, no. I'm…well, yes. I hate being cooped up on this ship while the captain is down there. He could be in trouble."

"He can take care of himself."

"I know, but it's embedded in me to protect the captain of the ship."

"What about everyone else?"

"I suppose that they have to protect him, too," Sandoo said with a shrug.

"No, I mean do you care about the others on the ship?"

"Oh, right. Yes, of course I do. It's not the same, though. My duty is first to the captain."

Geezer turned the final screw on the connection and opened a port to the operating system. He started working on the particulars of what he wanted this little evangelical *Ridgway Converter* to convince the transporter to do. If this worked, he'd be able to do all sorts of cool tech.

"So," he said as he coded, "if I were to be made captain, you'd feel that way about me?"

"I suppose so."

"What if Jezden were captain?"

"I'd resign."

"Smart," Geezer said with a nod. "You know, the best way you can keep the captain safe is to make sure the *Reluctant* is in tip-top shape when he gets back."

"Why would that matter?"

Geezer paused his work and gave Sandoo an odd look. "You were here when Frexle called. Someone in the Overseer group doesn't want us to succeed, and that means that they're going to do everything they can to make sure we don't. Remember what happens if we fail?"

"They'll destroy us all," Sandoo said with a grimace.

"Yep." Geezer picked back up on his coding. "That includes the captain."

"How am I supposed to protect the ship from that?"

"I'd say by helping the only person—other than the captain—on this crew who is capable of thinking outside of the box."

"You?"

"Me."

"Ah," Sandoo said slowly. "I'm now starting to see why you thought you were so highly ranked on this ship."

"Because I should be?"

"Precisely." Sandoo clapped his hands together and sighed in a very human way. "Okay, what can I do?"

"Leave me alone."

"Oh."

BATHROOM BUGS

*C*aptain Harr was standing in Dr. DeKella's bathroom. He hadn't had to actually go, which was great because he still wasn't quite sure how to navigate having a tail. That's when he noticed that the Kallian commodes weren't like Segnalian ones. These had no tank attached to the back. Rather, they had a channel, that he assumed was for a tail, that ran down the back of the seat. Interesting.

Why he'd really entered the bathroom, though, was because he felt that it was time to tell the good doctor what was really going on. She probably wouldn't believe him but, in the event that she did, he had to make sure that nobody else could overhear the admission. That meant he had to check for bugs, and that meant he had to contact Geezer to ask how exactly he would go about doing so. Ridly and the other androids were able to do this without using a wristband; Harr wasn't. So he needed some privacy before contacting his engineer. The only logical place ended up being the restroom since he had hopes that nobody would stick listening devices in there. If they did…well, that would be very disturbing indeed.

He pressed on his armband and activated the microscopic ear piece that Geezer had affixed to his eardrum. Then he put a call out.

"What's up, chief?"

"Hey, Geezer," he said quietly. "I'm in Dr. DeKella's bathroom at the moment."

"Kind of an odd place to call from."

"It's the only place I could go where nobody can hear me."

"Well," Geezer said pedantically, "I'm not much on human psychology, but I think one of the main reasons that you guys created the can was to give you a place where you could *go* without people hearing you."

"What are you talking about?" Harr said, but quickly realized precisely what Geezer thought was going on. "Oh, no, that's not what I meant. I don't have to relieve myself. I was looking for privacy because I need to make sure that Dr. DeKella's house isn't bugged."

"Ah, okay," Geezer said. "Glad to hear that, to be honest. I mean, I know we've grown kind of close since you jumped on the *Reluctant*, but—"

"Geezer," Harr interrupted, "how do I check for bugs?"

"Right. Well, activate your armband and scroll down through the list until you see an option that says, 'check for bugs' and then click it."

The font was so tiny that Harr had to squint through each item.

"Is there any way to zoom the text on this thing?" Harr asked.

"Actually, there's a really cool thing where you use your fingers in a pinching motion to zoom-in and zoom-out, but there's a galactic patent on the code so I couldn't use it."

"Great."

There were an incredible amount of options. Unfortunately, Geezer hadn't bothered to put them in any sensible order.

Signal for help
   Get the local time
   Find a restaurant
   Locate a lady of the night

"Locate a lady of the night?"

"Jezden."

Harr should have guessed. He scrolled to the next item.

"Find a pint of oil?"

"Unlike the rest of you, I need lubrication from time-to-time."

"Ah." He scrolled again. "You have a duplicate here, then."

"What?"

"You had 'Find a pint of oil,' right?"

"Yeah."

"The next item is, 'Find lubrication.'"

"Oh, that's another one of Jezden's."

Harr groaned and kept scrolling. Finally, he found the item and clicked it.

"Scanning…" the armband said in a female version of Geezer's voice. A tiny light moved back and forth along the band, changing from blue to green to yellow to red and back again. "There is an ant behind the toilet and a small collection of termites in the wall next to the shower."

"What?"

"Oh, sorry, chief," Geezer said. "You have to find the one that says, 'Check for *surveillance* bugs.'"

He did.

"Scanning…" The lightshow resumed for a few seconds longer this time. "There are no listening devices in this room."

"Sounds like it's clean, honcho."

"Indeed," Harr said. "Now I just have to figure out how I'm going to check the rest of the apartment."

"All the armband needs is a crack in the door and it'll scan, big cat."

Harr dropped to the floor and crawled over to the little gap under the door. He pressed the button and put the band as close to the opening as possible.

"Scanning…" He waited a bit longer than the previous two times. "Oh, yeah," the band said eventually, "that room is slammed with listening devices."

"Great," Harr said as he got back to his feet. "I guess I'll just have to get her to come in here. I'm sure that won't be awkward."

"Can't help you there, prime."

Getting her into the bathroom would be a trial, but once she realized everything that was going on, it would be brushed off. Hopefully. Part of him didn't like the idea of letting her in on what was really happening. He could just do the job, get out, and let her wonder for the rest of her days about why he'd disappeared. He just couldn't bring himself to do it. But he also knew that telling her that they weren't the actual inspectors was going to put a damper on their evening.

"Well, what's going on up there?" he asked Geezer.

"Where to start?" Geezer replied with his robotic sigh. "We tracked Vool like you asked. Sure enough, she was up to no good. Placed some charges in the lab. Ridly and Jezden have already disabled them."

"That's good."

"Sandoo and I got into a big discussion about the ranking

structure on the ship. Turns out I'm on par with Jezden. That was disturbing to learn."

"Only if you look at yourself as a soldier," Harr pointed out.

"Same thing Sandoo said, which has made me decide not to look at myself as a soldier. Though, frankly, I don't much look at Jezden as one, either."

"Tough to argue. What else?"

"That guy Frexle called to let us know that he thought Vool was planning to sabotage our plan to sabotage."

"He did what?"

"Yeah," Geezer replied. "We were perplexed as well. Apparently, Vool and some other Overseers want us to fail at this little mission, but Frexle is hoping we'll succeed."

"That's interesting." He hadn't expected any of them to really be on Platoon F's side, but it was nice to know that their boss was currently behind them. "Did he give us any useful insights?"

"Not really, other than it's becoming more and more obvious that a lot of their technology and vernacular seems to be paralleled in a number of Segnalian television shows."

"That might prove useful, especially since you appear to be an expert on many of those programs."

"I do love a good yarn, cap'n."

Harr was trying to think of a way to let Dr. DeKella get the full force of what was happening here. It could be that she would just take him at face value, but somehow he doubted that. More likely, she'd think he was nuts.

"Hey," he said with a snap of his fingers, "how's that beaming technology coming along?"

"That was next on my list, chief," Geezer replied. "I did some studying and found that I could hook in a *Ridgway Converter*."

"You mean that damn thing that made all the soda

machines on Segnal attempt to convert you to a Jelboobah's Witness?"

"Same one."

"I hope you have safeguards in place."

"Unless we have any Jelboobah's Witnesses on board, we should be safe. You tell the *Ridgway Converter* what brand of theology to sell, after all."

"Oh."

"Still, I put up a few blocks, just in case."

"Good. So it's working, then?"

"Seems to be. Haven't tried it on anything too large, but I sent out a box of tools and brought it back without any issues."

"Think it'll work on lifeforms?"

"Can't see why not."

Harr put his hands on the vanity and looked at himself in the mirror. That damned superhero chin of his was just as ridiculous as it had been when Admiral Parfait had commissioned it. At some point he would have to invest the time to have that corrected. The problem was that if he set that back to normal, he'd have to fix other things, too—most notably the wide jawline. That wouldn't be fun.

"Here's the thing," Harr said with a sigh. "I have to convince Dr. DeKella to help us. That's not going to be easy from here, but if I can transport her to our ship, she'd have no choice but to believe we're for real."

"I hear ya, honcho. It should work."

"You don't sound all that confident."

"My confidence level is moderate, I'll admit, but it'll improve a heck of a lot if you guys make it up here alive with all your parts in the right places."

"Swell."

UPDATING VELI

*V*eli was ravenous. Of course he was always ravenous. Even after a full meal of whatever creature he could sink his teeth into, he was always left wanting. It was in his nature.

What he was currently craving was to eat that traitor, Frexle. If only he could prove the worm to be a traitor, that is. Frexle had demonstrated himself to be very slippery indeed. It could be that he was actually innocent of the charges that Veli thought befitted the man, but somehow Veli doubted that. Frexle had pushed just a little too hard on this *HadItWithTheKillings* agenda. It was fishy, and Veli didn't like fish.

That thought made his stomach grumble again, reminding him that he did indeed like fish.

The phone rang. Veli glanced over and saw that it was Vool.

"Status?" he said after activating the call.

"Charges placed," she replied. "Ready to blow the crap out of this planet."

"Excellent," Veli said, his hunger somewhat sated by the

promise of violence. "We'll time it with the start of their test so it seems like an accident."

"Why does that matter? They'll all be dead anyway."

"The accident angle, Vool, is for the benefit of Frexle and his friends."

"Oh yeah, right. Damn liberals."

"Exactly. We should eat them all."

"What?" she said while wrinkling her nose.

"Kill them all," he amended quickly. "I meant that we should kill them all."

"Oh."

"Where are you going to be when you activate the charges?"

"In the building, obviously."

Veli blinked in disbelief at the screen. Not that she could see him. He never allowed anyone to see him. Being the Lord Overseer was a risky proposition at best, but offering would-be assassins—such as Vool—to see what he looked like was akin to signing your own death warrant. Plus, if the rest of the Overseers knew what Veli truly was, they'd not likely want to keep him in power. So, he stayed ever in the shadows, and never in the spot where a shooter would expect him to be, either.

"I'll leave right before I hit the *boom* button."

"Oh," Veli said. He'd hoped that she wouldn't catch on to the fact that by being in the building during the explosion, she was sealing her own fate. He shrugged. "What are your plans until then?"

"I guess I'll watch some television or something," she said with a shrug. "I'm sure it'll be boring. What I'd like to do is go out and do a little hunting."

"Now, now," Veli cautioned, "I need you to hang tight, Vool. We don't want to tip our hat too soon. Remember, tomorrow you'll have the lives of billions at your fingertips. Just hang on to that for tonight."

"Whatever."

"Any news on the tech on that ship?"

"No, that metal dork wouldn't give me any information on it."

"Metal dork?"

"Yeah, that walking dishwasher that works in engineering."

"Damn," said Veli. "Well, once you get through blowing up that measly little planet, you can focus on getting me that intel."

AIDING JEZDEN

*T*ry as she might, Ridly couldn't keep focused on her studies. She knew it was silly, since the technology was doomed to fail anyway—that being the purpose for Platoon F's arrival to Kallian—but she couldn't help but be interested in how the warp tech worked. It was clear that whoever handled Ridly's programming had added a healthy dose of curiosity to her code.

Silly or not, it was pointless to even try to comprehend what the Kallians were doing because all she could hear was Jezden's constant moaning and groaning.

"Okay, okay," she said, slamming down the massive book she'd been reading, "stop the sighing already. It's getting on my nerves."

"Sorry," he said with another sigh. "I guess I can't even do that right."

She rolled her eyes and then glared up at the ceiling. "Ugh. All right, out with it."

"What?"

"I'm trying to study here," she said, motioning toward the

desk, "and you're making that impossible, so just get whatever it is off your chest so I can get back to work."

He looked away. "It's not important."

"It's the small-tail thing again, isn't it?" she said. "You know I'm just giving you crap about it so that you can get a dose of your own medicine, right?"

"Still hurts."

"As it does to everyone else when you're being...well, you."

"Thanks," Jezden said sadly. "That helps. I feel much better now. Glad you're here."

"What does it matter about the damned tail anyway? It's not even real."

"I know it's not real, but everyone on this stupid planet thinks it is."

"So?"

"So they're not looking past it," he said with his hands up. "I mean, I'm an exceptionally good-looking guy, you know?"

"You're certainly always the first to point that out, so there must be something to it."

"Right?" he said as if trying to convince her. "Seriously, look at me. I'm *really* good looking."

"Yeah, yeah, yeah," Ridly said, having a difficult time thinking otherwise. He *was* ridiculously attractive...on the outside.

"But nobody seems to care about that," he said, slumping again. "They just look at my tail—my *one* flaw—and they don't even give the real me a chance."

"To be fair," Ridly said as compassionately as she could manage, "the real you is a total asshole, Jezden."

"Again, thanks for the support."

"Look, I'm sorry, but it's true. You were programmed to be a chauvinistic weasel whose only purpose is to get laid. I have no idea why you were made that way, but you were."

"And I can't help how I was made, can I?"

"No," she admitted, "I suppose not."

"Yet you all judge me for it constantly. Do I judge you for being made smart, confident, and pretty?"

She jerked her head toward him. "You think I'm pretty?"

"The point," he continued, ignoring her question, "is that I don't pick on you because you're brainy."

"Actually, you do it all the time."

Again, he ignored her response. "I just don't understand how anyone could discard a person just because of the length of their tail."

"Fine," she said as she flipped open her datapad, "let's find out." She hooked into the Kallian version of the Internet and began her search. "Okay, it says here that the length of a Kallian's tail has been shown as a direct connection to how well they perform in both the bedroom and the conference room. A longer tail signifies virility and power. All high-ranking officials have longer tails. Low-level workers tend to have short tails. Middle management…"

"Medium-sized tails," Jezden interrupted. "Right, I get it. I'm not *that* dumb."

There was more detail regarding the tail situation, but she didn't think he'd care, so she shut down the pad. "Bottom line is that you just screwed yourself by demanding a smaller tail."

"Obviously."

"But who cares, Jezden?" she said. "Soon enough we'll be off this planet and you'll be the talk of the town again."

"Yeah, I guess so."

"Now," she said as she stared longingly at the stack of books that were calling to her, "can we get back to the part where you said I was pretty?"

SPY BLOCK

*W*hy didn't you bug the bathroom, Ewups?"

"Uh," Ewups said with a look of disgust, "because it would be gross, sir."

"I guess it would, at that."

Private Deddles walked in the main door, having returned from his trip to the lab. He'd been gone for the better part of an hour. Why it took him so long to refashion some simple wires, Struggins couldn't say, other than noting that the boy was about as useful as a pair of cloth combat boots.

"You got the wires fixed, Deddles?"

"Yes, sir."

"Good. That should surprise those 'inspectors,'" he said, making air quotes with his fingers.

"I thought they weren't really inspectors, sir?" Deddles replied.

"They're not. That's why I used air quotes, Private."

Deddles appeared confused.

Kids these days, thought Struggins with a shake of his head as he walked over to the window that overlooked the lab.

He blamed the media more than anything else. They were the ones pushing television and video games at the younger generation. It had gotten to the point where there just wasn't any creativity anymore. All the damn kids ever did was to stare at a box that hypnotized them and sold them on the sugary-snacks-and-fizzy-drinks diet. Granted, he liked to have a beer now and then, and he wasn't quite as tight around the middle as he was in his youth, but for a man approaching 75, he was pretty damn fit. The youth of today, though, were overweight, easily bored, lacking in creative pursuits, and they'd lost that respect for elders that he'd learned growing up. To prove his point, he had three obnoxious grandchildren who fit that mold perfectly.

Now, Deddles wasn't overweight and he probably wasn't much at video games either, except maybe for *Dot and Paddles* —a game that even monkeys were able to master without much fuss. But Deddles just didn't get it. Hardly any of them did. At least not like the recruits when Struggins was young.

That thought dropped him into a memory of his first day at Camp Klikmore. Everyone on the bus heading to camp was nervous, but in a good way. It was a glorious day for them all. They were going to be a part of something. To serve. To fight. To kill, if needed, yes, but only soldiers who were on the other side, and that was okay because those soldiers were trying to kill you back.

He'd never forget rushing off that bus as Drill Sergeant Lorgen screamed at them like they were vermin. Lorgen had been simultaneously the most hated and revered man of Struggins' illustrious military career. During his entire stay at Camp Klikmore, Lorgen berated him, yelled at him, made him do push-ups, sit-ups, and laps. He had him peel potatoes, tear down and clean weapons, and scrub latrines. Never once did he treat Struggins or any of the recruits with kid gloves. They were in the military and that meant something. The only nice thing Lorgen had ever said to him was on the day of graduation, and it was, "You're graduating from 'shit on a shoe' to 'piss on the rim of the can', Struggins. If you make beyond that, I'll be amazed." Struggins smiled at the memory of that statement. It wasn't much, but those were the most powerful words that he'd ever heard.

Lorgen was a 20-Star General now. Shit on the shoe for him these days was most likely self-inflicted. Struggins had seen him often at command headquarters downtown, but he never said anything to his former drill instructor. Mostly because he was afraid that Lorgen might recognize him and make him do 100 push-ups. More so, though, because he was afraid that Lorgen may no longer have the faculties to be that larger-than-life figure he had been when Struggins stepped off that bus in Camp Klikmore.

"Sir," Ewups announced, jolting Struggins from his thoughts.

"Hmmm?"

"Dr. Welder is exiting the bathroom."

"It's about damn time."

THE NIGHTIE

*H*arr had fully intended to be businesslike about this ordeal, but sometimes intentions got clouded when facing a woman who was wearing a nightie. Well, to be more accurate, Dr. DeKella was wearing almost nothing at all. The nightie concept was a little bit of lace over her hands, feet, and ears, which was obviously what Kallians considered to be lingerie. To Harr, what he was seeing was a well-developed feminine form in the nude, and she had all the bells and whistles.

The concept of sticking to business was getting…harder.

But he fought his primal urges, took a deep breath, focused his mind, and said, "Glug."

"I take it you like what you see?" she said while batting her eyelashes.

"Umbah," he replied stoically.

"I'm hoping that at least negligees are the same where you're from, yes?"

He nodded dumbly. They weren't at all like what he was seeing, but the brain in charge of him at the moment was the one housed snuggly in his trousers, and it knew only one mode of logic: agree with whatever the naked girl is telling you.

SPY INTEREST

"What the hell do you mean you didn't put cameras in her apartment?" General Struggins shrieked.

"Yeah," agreed Private Deddles with equal ferocity.

"That would be spying, sir," Ewups offered in poor defense.

"What the hell do you think the bugs are for, Ewups?"

"Good point, sir."

"Damn it!" said Deddles while kicking one of the desk legs.

"Settle down, Deddles," Struggins warned, though he couldn't blame the private for his outburst in this instance. "Any chance we can rig one of the cameras from the W.A.R.P.E.D. building exterior to peek into her window?"

"Honestly, sir?"

Struggins grimaced and then kicked the same desk leg that Deddles had kicked. "Damn it."

COME WITH ME

*A*re you just going to stand there, Dr. Welder?" she said as her breasts swayed in hypnotic fashion.

He had to fight this. First of all, he had absolutely zero idea how to please a Kallian woman. He barely knew how to please a Segnalian one.

Apparently, this thought triggered the ocular device that Geezer had outfitted him with, because two seconds later, there was a three-dimensional representation of all of her sensual parts highlighted in his visual field. That could prove useful, assuming he could get himself interested in the various items listed, which included preening her ear hair, nibbling on the fleshy spot between her forefinger and thumb, and making whooping noises while he jumped around and clapped. Thinking about these things gave his top-side brain just enough of an edge to regain control of the situation. Another glance at her breasts, though, started an internal tug-o-war.

He had to act fast.

"Listen," he said, tearing his eyes away, "I know this is

going to sound really odd, but would you join me in the bathroom?"

The silence was such that Harr had to look at her again to make sure that she was still breathing. Her mouth hung open and the look on her face was a mixture of shock, fear, and disappointment. He replayed his last sentence over in his head and concluded that he would have given her the same look had their roles been reversed. Then again, if he had breasts like that, he'd probably just stand in front of a full-length mirror all day while admiring himself.

"I'm sorry," DeKella replied, "did you just ask me to go into the bathroom with you?"

"I know that sounds really...odd, but believe me, it'll be worth it."

"I don't know, Zep," she said. "I'm not really into that kinky stuff. I mean, I thought that your interest in breasts was weird enough, but this is a little much." Somewhat thankfully, she grabbed her robe and slid it on, which allowed Harr's main brain to secure a solid foothold. "I like you, Zep. I really do." She crossed her arms and shook her head. "This is just too weird for me."

"I really need you to trust me on this, Rella," he said gently. "I promise that it's not what you think. Honestly." She seemed to be weighing things. "If you feel uncomfortable at all, once we're in there, you can leave and that will be that."

She stared at him for a few more moments before dropping her hands. "Okay, Zep," she said, "I'll trust you. But you have to promise to take things slow."

"I promise."

"And if I say, 'Wacky wacky wham!' at any time, you have to stop whatever it is we're doing."

It was Harr's turn to give the "Huh?" look. "What does 'Wacky wacky wham!' mean?"

"That's my safe-word."

"It's more like three words."

"Actually," she mused, "you're right. Never thought of that. Anyway, are we agreed?"

"We are."

"Well, then," DeKella said with an audible gulp, "let's go into the bathroom."

SPY DISINTEREST

*G*ood call on not installing cameras, Ewups," Struggins said with a shudder. "I really don't want to see whatever is about to happen next."

"No, sir."

"Wherever this guy is *really* from, they obviously have some pretty strange mating rituals." Struggins had a couple of skeletons in his closet, of course—everyone did—but nothing like what this "inspector" was up to. "I just don't understand people these days," he said. "When I was young, we did the normal things like hand-nibbling, ear-hair preening, and yelling 'whoop' while jumping around and clapping our hands."

Deddles obviously saw this as a chance to offer his two cents, much to the chagrin of both Struggins and Ewups. "There are movies out these days where the men like legs and the women like biceps."

"That's disgusting," Ewups said.

"Keep your dirty movies to yourself, Private. Nobody wants to hear about your moronic perversions."

"They're not mine, sir! I was just…"

"Too late to back out now, Deddles," Struggins said. "Bad enough that a man spouts out obscene images like that, but then not to own up to his own personal interests? Well, that's just unforgivable."

"But I don't like that stuff, sir. I was just…"

"I think you've said enough, Deddles," Struggins cut him off. "And I sure hope you washed your hands before bringing our food earlier."

Private Deddles just sat down and groaned.

SPILLING THE BEANS

Okay," DeKella said, "just tell me when I can open my eyes."

"You didn't have to close them in the first place," Harr replied. She opened them as he shut the door. "I have to tell you something that's not going to be easy for you to hear."

"You mean there's something worse than you wanting to have sex in the bathroom?"

Harr cracked his neck from side to side. "Rella, are you aware that your house is bugged?"

"Oh!" She began laughing. She reached out her hand and pressed it against Harr's shoulder for a moment. "So that's what this is about?"

"Partially."

"Zep," she said as she wiped her eyes, "I try to keep things clean, but they show up anyway. I think it's the neighbors downstairs. Those people are slobs. The exterminator comes out once a month, but …"

"Sorry, Rella, I'm not talking about insects. I'm talking about surveillance bugs."

"I don't understand."

"Listening devices," he explained. "They're all over your house."

Dr. DeKella appeared more confused now than when Harr had asked her to join him in the bathroom. This, in turn, confused Harr.

"What are you talking about, Zep?"

"You really don't know, do you?" She shook her head in response. "Rella, you said that the military was highly interested in this warp technology, right?"

"Of course."

"And do you know what that means?"

"That they want to use the technology?" she asked as if he were stupid.

"It means that they're going to make sure everything goes according to plan," he stated, "and that means that they're going to spy on everyone involved in the program."

"Spying?" she said as if she had just been slapped. "That's ridiculous. People don't spy on people here on Kallian."

"I'm afraid they do, Rella," Harr replied.

By now she had crossed her arms again. At any moment he was afraid she'd say, "Wacky wacky wham!" and leave the room. Fortunately, she again gave him the benefit of the doubt and said, "Where's your proof, Zep?"

Harr showed her the armband, first pointing out its capabilities by giving her the updated location of the ant that was now climbing along the side of her clothes' hamper, and the termites that had clearly been happy enough in their original location. Once he swept the bathroom for listening devices, showing none, the result of the outer room search was most impactful.

"I can't believe it," she said as she removed the pieces of lingerie from her ears, hands, and feet, "those bastards have no right to spy on me."

"No, they don't," Harr agreed, "but you're the head of the

very project that they desperately want to see succeed, and so they're doing what they can to make sure nothing stands in their way. It's how the military operates."

"You seem to know a lot about how the military works, 'Dr. Welder.'"

He took a deep breath. Here is where things were really going to get interesting. She'd either believe him or throw him out. At least he had already shown that the military *was* spying on her, which would serve to give him some credibility.

"My name is not Zep Welder," he admitted, "and I'm not an inspector. Hell, I'm not even a doctor."

"Son of a bitch," she said, reaching for the door.

"Please hear me out," he pleaded. "I've already shown you that you're being spied on. And I didn't have to tell you that." She paused but didn't look back. "What's the worst that can happen? You listen and that's it. If you don't believe me, then turn me in and let me suffer the consequences." She let go of the doorknob. "I know this is all overwhelming, but I can assure you it's about to get worse."

"I'm not sure how it can," she said without looking back.

"I'm not from your planet."

Her shoulders visibly slumped. She slowly turned around to face him. Her gaze wasn't exactly one that was angry, but it wasn't jolly either.

"I really should have listened to my mother," she said with a shake of her head. "My soon-to-be ex-husband was a self-involved jerk, but at least he wasn't crazy. Every date I go on just proves time and time again that my ex wasn't as bad as I'd thought."

Harr struggled through. "I know this makes me sound like a lunatic, but I honestly am from another planet, and I can prove it."

"I have an idea," she said in an over-the-top way, "how

about I call the friendly people who drive the little white vans around? When they come to pick you up and give you some pretty pills, you can tell them all about your space adventure. I'm sure you'll be a hit down at the happy farm."

"Just humor me, will you?"

"Actually, I probably should. I've read that we should always play nice with the criminally insane."

"I haven't done anything criminal."

"Where are the real inspectors?" she challenged him with one eyebrow on the rise.

Damn. He tapped on his wrist band. "Geezer?"

"Still here, chief."

"Interesting," DeKella said, clearly unable to hear the conversation going on with the robot. "Do all aliens talk to their wristbands, or is it just those from your planet?"

He frowned at her. "Geezer, transport me up."

"You sure about that, cap'n?"

"The better question is: are *you* sure it's going to work?"

"I don't know," he said. "I'd guess it would, though. This *Ridgway Converter* is quite convincing."

He peered up at DeKella, who had her damned arms crossed again. "Activate it."

"Okay," Geezer said with a voice that sounded like it carried a shrug along with it. "Just in case, chief, it's been nice knowing ya. For a captain, you weren't a complete pain in my ass."

"Gee, thanks."

"No, seriously. I've had a lot of captains over the years. Some were total jerks and the rest were even worse. You're different. It's like you have a level of patience with me that nobody else..."

"Just press the damn button, will you?" Harr commanded as his nerve began to wane.

"Fine," Geezer replied angrily, "but I take back all that nice crap I just said."

The world suddenly started to look a bit fuzzy and his skin began to itch terribly. It didn't hurt so much as tickle. This lasted about three seconds before Dr. DeKella slowly faded away. The look on her face was exactly what Harr was hoping for. If she didn't believe him now, she never would.

When everything faded back in, Harr found that he was standing in the engineering room of the *Reluctant*.

"Unbelievable," he said as he studied his hands and feet.

"Wow," Geezer said. "It actually worked. You feel all right?"

"I think so." Harr took a few moments to walk around, touch some panels and desks to make sure it was all real, and to take some calming breaths. "I'm a little jittery, but that's probably just due to being the first Segnalian to ever have gone through something like that."

"Yes!" Geezer did a little fist-pump. "Another fine win for the G.3.3.Z.3.R. line."

"I have to hand it to you, Geezer," Harr said while patting the robot on the shoulder, "you truly are amazing...ly lucky."

"Luck is the result of hard work, big cat. You should know that."

Harr nodded. "Hard work slapping random pieces together and hiding under the desk while flipping switches?"

"In this body?" Geezer replied. "You know it, boyo."

"Right. Seeing that you transported me up safely enough, what say we bring up the lovely Dr. DeKella next?"

"You sure she's okay with that?" Geezer asked.

"Let's find out."

The robot shrugged and reached for his datapad. "You're the boss."

A few moments later, a screaming Dr. DeKella was standing

in the engineering room looking as though she'd seen a ghost. Harr reached out and rubbed her shoulders to try and calm her down. It seemed to be arousing her instead. He focused on his HUD and noted that it was yet another erogenous zone.

"Rella," Harr said gently while pulling his hands away, "listen to me."

"Wacky wacky wham! Wacky wacky wham!"

"Dr. DeKella," he said more sternly, grabbing her by the elbows, which was not on the list of Kallian play parts, "you're going to have to get a hold of yourself." She was on the brink of hyperventilation. "Listen to me," Harr continued firmly, "I know that this is a lot to take in, but you can handle it."

"Sounds like something Jezden would say," noted Geezer, just loud enough for only Harr to hear.

"What the hell is happening?" Her voice was a ragged whisper. "Have I lost my mind?"

"Not yet," Harr answered. "You're on my ship, Rella. We're currently orbiting above your planet."

"That's not possible." Her eyes were darting about. "We would have seen you."

"Nah, ladybug," Geezer said, causing her to jump and shriek again. "We're cloaked."

She pointed at Geezer in horror. "Talking metal…" was all she could muster before her eyes rolled up into her head and she keeled over. Fortunately, Harr caught her just before she hit the floor.

"That went well," Geezer said.

"I'm going to carry her up to the bridge."

"Use my lift," Geezer suggested, pointing to the mini elevator by the far wall. "It'll be easier."

"Good idea."

SPY CONCERN

*A*ll Kallian buildings had built-in life sensors. It was not considered a means of spying, but rather a way to make sure that nobody was in distress. The *Lifeform Reader*, or *LFR*, as they were called, didn't pay any attention to what the lifeform in question was actually up to, but rather just verified if they were registering still as a lifeform at all. In other words, if a person died, the *LFR* would know about it and would send out an urgent message to the local hospital. This wasn't all that helpful in the grand scheme of things, considering that the *LFR* could only manage to judge between life and death. If the person died, the emergency response crews arriving on the scene couldn't do much but take the body away. Eventually, the *LFR* systems were instead tied directly to the morgue network, being that it was a more efficient protocol. It was reported that the company who pioneered the *LFR* was working on a new model, called the *LF Distress Reader*, which could detect signs of extreme discomfort as well. Their initial tests showed too many dispatches to homes where people had recently eaten at *Taco Gong* or had tried out the various forms of kink mentioned in the best-selling *Fifty-Three Shades of*

White, though. Anyone who has ever eaten at *Taco Gong* was bound to have a few restroom visits that would register on the *LFDR*, and anyone who was interested in *Fifty-Three Shades of White* were probably just plain bound.

"What do you mean there's only one lifeform registering in the bathroom now? How's that possible?"

"Maybe they're, uh, merging, sir," Ewups answered.

"It only reads one lifeform when people do that?" Struggins asked, greatly confused by the technician's lack of knowledge on a subject that he should be an expert on. Not the subject of merging, of course, but rather the subject of how the *LFR* readings actually worked.

"I guess so," said Ewups. "I've never scanned people who were in the middle of relations before, and it's not like they have the *LFDR* installed, sir."

Struggins grunted.

"Wait," Ewups said while typing something on his machine. "Now it's showing that nobody is in that room."

"That's not possible," Struggins said with a huff. "Obviously your equipment is malfunctioning."

"No, sir," Ewups answered with a firm shake of his head. "I just had it checked at the urologist last week because things haven't been so great between me and the missus. He said I have the body of a thirty-five year old."

"But you're only twenty-two," said Deddles.

"I'm talking about the surveillance equipment," Struggins stated. "Your connection to the *LFR* is clearly screwed up. Idiots."

"Oh, right." Ewups started typing faster than any person should be capable of. Rows and rows of gobbledygook flew down his screen as Struggins gazed in wonder. Ewups ran his finger back and forth over the incoming data as if he were reading a novel. "No, I don't think that's it."

"How can you be sure?"

"Because it's still picking up readings on an ant and a colony of termites."

Struggins brought his hand to his chin. Something else had to be going on here. *LFR*s may be mostly pointless, but they rarely failed.

Maybe these "inspectors" were some type of undercover task force sent in to kidnap DeKella so that they could get all of the secrets on the warp technology for themselves. But who would even do that? There was only one military in all of Kallian. It could be terrorists, of course, were there any. The last terrorist group to exist was wiped out during the *Raid of Gipany* over twenty years ago. A few start-ups tried to follow, but they were easily squashed. Obviously, there could be a new group that was just up and coming and not yet on the radar. If so, they were certainly well-funded and very good at their jobs.

"Where the hell could they be?" Struggins said softly, more to himself than to Ewups.

"I don't know, sir. It's like they've vanished."

He hated not having eyes on a situation that needed eyes. Being in the dark was not something that a general in the Kallian Military was accustomed to. That meant he had no other options but to send in the cavalry.

"Deddles," he said calmly, "mobilize the stealth soldiers and get them into Dr. DeKella's house, on the double."

"Now, sir?"

"Yes, Private, now."

"I will need to get the forms, sir," Deddles said as he sat down at one of the computers and looked at it dumbly. "Does anyone know how to get the forms from here?"

"Deddles," Struggins said, closing his eyes, "we don't have time to fill out any forms. This is an emergency situation.

You just need to mobilize the stealth soldiers as I have just requested you to do."

"But, sir…"

"You can tell them that it is under the direct order of General Struggins. I will worry about cleaning up the mess later." And he would do so by having Deddles clean up the mess later.

"Are you sure, because…"

Struggins felt his calm break. He yanked Deddles from the chair, grabbed the front of his uniform and began shaking him as he screamed, "Mobilize! Mobilize!"

SEEING KALLIAN

*I*t had taken Dr. DeKella a little while to calm down after regaining consciousness. Harr had seated her in the Captain's chair on the bridge of the *SSMC Reluctant*. He had introduced her to Sandoo, Moon, Middleton, and Curr, though he was careful to hold back the fact that they were all androids, as he wasn't sure she could handle that at the moment. How she'd reacted to Geezer was bad enough.

On the screen was the floating image of Kallian. Harr could only imagine how she felt seeing her world from this perspective. He had grown up in an era where viewing planets from outer space was old hat to even the common man. On Kallian, though, it was only the chosen few who had been given this privilege.

"That's your home planet, Rella."

"It's amazing." She was barely audible. "There just aren't any words."

He knelt down beside her and took her hand in his, carefully avoiding the little webbing between her forefinger and thumb.

"We have to talk, Rella," he said gently.

231

She turned and looked at him with shock in her eyes. "This isn't one of those it's-not-you-it's-me conversations, is it?"

"What?"

"I mean, it's not like we've really got anything going on yet. Granted, you were at my house and you somehow managed to convince me to have sex with you in the bathroom,"—the androids spun around and gave him a disturbed look— "and even though it turned out that you weren't trying to have sex with me in the bathroom," —the androids un-grimaced and turned back to their stations— "I was still *willing* to do that because I thought we had something special going on here."

"So do I," Harr said, relieved that she felt the same way.

"Then why do we need to talk? Nothing good ever comes from the 'we need to talk' talk. I know because I've had many of those talks."

"I'm sorry," Harr said. She was obviously still in a heap of mental confusion, so he had to choose his words carefully. "We were sent to your planet for a very specific reason."

"Is it bad?"

"It's not great," he admitted with a frown. "You see, we were sent by a highly intelligent race—according to them— that believes your society is progressing to a point where you could be a threat to them some day."

"Some day? Like in a week, or a year, or what?"

"Honestly, Rella, I haven't a clue how they calculate these things. I just know that if that warp test of yours succeeds tomorrow, they're going to destroy your planet."

She sat up straight. "You can't be serious."

"We're in a spaceship, Rella. I'm not sure what more I can do to show you how serious I am."

"Shit," she said while pushing herself out of the chair as if looking for a way to escape. It was obvious to Harr that she was about to pass out again, so he jumped over and grabbed her before she could fall.

"What happened?" Sandoo said. "Is she okay?"

"She's just dizzy," Harr replied. "You know how it is with people being on a ship for the first time."

"Not really," Sandoo said.

"My guess is something inner-ear."

"We have a bathroom she could use, if that will help?"

Harr tilted his head at Sandoo. Then he rolled his eyes and said it very slowly this time. "*Inner ear*, Commander."

"Oh!" Sandoo nodded. "You mean her cochlear fluids are imbalanced. I see now. I thought you meant…"

"I know, I know. Easy to misunderstand. Let it go."

Finally, Dr. DeKella closed her eyes and steadied herself. "What do we do?"

Harr hated to have to answer that question, but there really was no other way around it. They couldn't be allowed to succeed. Not only for the sake of Kallian, but also for the sake of his crew and ship.

"The test has to fail, Rella."

"But…"

"I know how you feel," Harr stated before she could start, "and believe me when I say that I have absolutely no personal desire to see your life's work go down the toilet, but these people mean business. If we don't flub up that test, Kallian is going to be a lot less spherical come tomorrow afternoon."

"Wow."

"This has to be a lot to process, and I'm sorry that you're involved in all of this."

"Like you said," she said quietly, "I'm in charge of the project. Matter of circumstance." Harr gave her a few minutes to process everything. Eventually, she said, "Well, how do we proceed?"

"*You* have to tell me that," Harr answered. "I need a way to stop that test from succeeding. Hopefully without anyone getting hurt."

"Okay," she said, nodding. "We just have to block the *Stewnathium Particles* from getting to the Multicombo Chamber."

"That's it?"

"Yes."

"Will that be catastrophic enough?" Harr asked. "This has to be one of the epic failures that can't be recovered from, Rella. In other words, your reputation, career, and everything have to be completely tarnished from this. You have to be made to look the fool so that nobody can easily pick up where you left off. They have to drop this project completely."

"Right," she said stoically. "Okay, so I'll introduce in *Layzo Atoms*. They'll interact with the mixture in the chamber and cause a full meltdown, assuming that the *Stewnathium Particles* don't make it through. It just has to look like they did, and that those particles are what caused the meltdown."

"Got it," Harr affirmed. "How do we stop them?"

"Someone from your team will have to be in the room above the lab. There's an access portal on the side of the housing for the particles. They'll need to insert a *Claythom Pole* into the main port and that will block the flow."

"And this pole is in that room?"

"It will be," she said. "I'll hide it behind one of the pillars. You'll just have to be sure that those particles don't get through."

"Understood," Harr said. "If they get through, then your test will succeed, and that..."

"No," she interrupted, "not with *Layzo Atoms* in the mix. If the particles get through, it'll cause the building to explode."

"What?"

"I need the *Layzos* in there to melt down the chamber, but

if you mix *Layzos* with *Stewnathium Particles*, you're going to have a very bad day."

"I see," said Harr as he rubbed his superhero chin. "Well, let's get back down to your bathroom and get things rolling. We don't have a lot of time."

She ogled the main screen and said, "May I have one last look at my Kallian before we go?"

"Of course," Harr said, motioning her back to his chair. "Actually, Lieutenant Moon, would you do our guest the kindness of flying her completely around the planet, please?"

"Certainly, thir."

'COME TO VELI' MEETING

*T*he job as a whole wasn't bad, considered Frexle. In fact, it was pretty decent when you considered the perks that came along with it. But reporting to Veli was a dicey proposition, and the Lord Overseer had demanded another meeting. It wasn't Veli's style to *request* anything.

Fortunately, Veli wasn't eating this time.

"There's a rumor going around that *you* are the head of this *HadItWithTheKillings* group, Frexle," Veli said gratingly. "Is this true?"

Frexle fought to keep himself calm. Being accused of such a thing could be a death sentence. There was no 'innocent until proven guilty' rule in the land of the Overseers, after all. Of course, he was essentially facing his demise anyway since Veli had all but decided that Platoon F was going to fail, hence the real reason he'd sent Vool. There was still hope that the crew would succeed, and that had given Frexle enough to hang onto…until now.

"I cannot tell a lie, Lord Overseer," he said, thinking on his feet, "for if I did, you would most certainly know it."

"Yes, I would." His words were laced with accusation.

"Of course you would," Frexle agreed confidently. He had an angle. "Your intellect knows no bounds, my lord."

"That's true."

"Again, Lord Overseer, I can only speak the truth when in your presence. To do otherwise would be naught but a foolhardy pursuit."

"I'll grant you that," Veli said, "and since you are obviously aware of this fact, I'll ask you again: Are you the head of this pesky group?"

"I am not, my lord."

"Really?" Veli said, sounding shocked. "Damn. I thought certain that I had that one nailed down." Frexle held his tongue as Veli tapped on his desk with what sounded like an ice pick. "But seeing that you couldn't possibly speak falsehoods around me, after your incredibly accurate description of my intellect and all, I suppose I have little choice but to believe you."

Frexle fought the desire to take a deep breath and say, "Whew." His life had been waiting behind the curtain just moments before, preparing itself to flash before his eyes. Fortunately, there was another rain check. At least until it was learned if Platoon F had succeeded or not.

"Your wisdom is supreme, Lord Overseer. I take comfort knowing that my innocence was the only conclusion your advanced mind could have arrived at."

"Exactly," Veli agreed. "Ah well, I guess it's some *other* idiot. I'll just have to keep an eye out."

"Yes, sir."

"Have *you* heard any updates from Vool lately?"

"No, sir. I assumed she was only contacting you directly since there is little point in her going to one of your underlings."

"True again." Veli's clicking on the table was now moving in rapid hits. Frexle had noticed that the Lord Overseer tended to do that when he was feeling important or pleased. "I have to say, Frexle, that your perfect evaluation of *my* incredibleness serves to improve my position on *your* acumen."

"That must mean that I'm not nearly as stupid as many people think, my lord. I am fortunate that the greatest mind the Overseers have ever been privileged to call their leader has formally declared me as intelligent."

"I never said that," Veli retorted. The clicking stopped. "I'm just saying that you're not a *complete* moron."

"That's enough to brighten my day, my lord."

"Understandable." Back to a single tap every few seconds. "Anyway, what's the latest on this warp test?"

"It's still on as scheduled, my lord."

"That should be an interesting light show," Veli said happily. "Yes, yes, nothing better than blowing things up, except maybe eating things that are struggling not to be eaten." Frexle couldn't contain a shudder. "Also enjoy those plagues. They're a hoot."

"As you say, sir."

"Well, it seems that you're not the leader of that group, so your death will have to wait until this crew of yours fails tomorrow."

"Great…sir."

SPY RUN

$\mathcal{T}$echnician Ewups had rigged it up so that General Struggins could see through the goggles of his lead trooper as the team of soldiers closed in on DeKella's apartment, which took them an incredible fifteen minutes to manage. They slid through the main lobby without much fuss, except for a little dog that kept barking at them as they waited for the elevator. The apartment building was only three levels, so Struggins couldn't fathom why they hadn't just taken the stairs. Then again, the out-of-breath sounds coming from the small band of black-clad soldiers spelled that they were struggling enough with just the run in to the building.

The elevator doors opened and they began moving in, but an old lady was already inside the elevator.

"Out of the way, you hoodlums," she said. "You let people *out* of the elevator before you go *in*. Kids these days just don't have any respect for the way of things."

"Sorry, grandma."

"Grandma? I'm not your grandma." The old lady was suddenly brandishing an umbrella because, well, that's what old ladies tended to do when they felt irritable. "I've a mind to knock you upside that silly helmet of yours, I do."

"Quick, everyone inside."

Struggins heard a "dink" sound that spelled the old lady had indeed knocked his lead trooper upside the head as they piled into the elevator.

"Should I assume," Struggins said through the microphone, "that your team isn't well-versed with stealth, Sergeant Clebsy?"

"Only the 'wearing dark clothes' part, sir. We've just recently graduated from that class. We would have been out sooner, but Lieutenant Zjarba kept on donning bright green socks, so…"

"I don't need the details, Sergeant," Struggins said tiredly. "What I need is for you and your team to try to be as quiet as you can when you get to DeKella's room. We don't want to tip our hand."

"Ricky that, sir," said the remote soldier.

"Isn't that supposed to be 'Roger that,' sir?" Private Deddles asked.

Struggins covered the microphone. "Clebsy's ex-husband's name was Roger, and she hates his guts, so she refuses to use his name in any context."

"Oh."

Clebsy attached a card to the electronic reader on the door. A couple of seconds later, the light turned green and she turned the handle to reveal DeKella's apartment. Struggins grunted upon noticing that the place was nicer than his.

"Again," he warned, "keep quiet."

"Yes, sir."

"You just said that at full voice, Clebsy. You need to whisper."

"Sorry, sir," she said at full volume.

Honestly! He counted to ten and then centered himself.

"Slip toward the bathroom," he commanded, "and tell me if you see any shadows."

"The bathroom, sir?"

"Again, will you please whisper?"

"Sorry, sir."

"Yes," Struggins affirmed, "the bathroom."

"Why are they in the bathroom together, sir?"

"First off, we don't even know if they *are* in the bathroom. Secondly, if they happen to be, you don't want to know why. Trust me on that."

"Ricky that, sir."

Clebsy motioned the other soldiers to check the rest of the apartment while she headed for the bathroom. There was a light coming from under the door, but there was no way to tell if anyone was inside. Struggins couldn't see any shadows moving or anything.

The sound of a bag ruffling suddenly filled the air.

Crunch.

"What the hell was that?" Struggins asked.

Chomp, chomp, chomp.

Clebsy started seeking out the source of the crunching sounds. Struggins was hopeful that the moronic soldiers wouldn't be caught, but if they were he would simply deny any involvement and instead pin it on one of the local police chiefs.

Crunch. Chomp, chomp, chomp.

Clebsy turned the corner to the kitchen, her gun held high, when she saw Private Upler with his hand in a bag of chips.

"What the hell is he doing?" Struggins said.

"What the hell are you doing?" Clebsy nearly mimicked.

"I was hungry," Upler replied and then offered her the bag. "Want some?"

"Sure," Clebsy replied, reaching her hand in.

"Stop," Struggins yelled. "This is unbelievable. Put those damn chips away right now or I'll have you both put in irons."

Clebsy yanked her hand out of the bag and then wagged a finger at Upler. "You should know better, soldier," she said. "We're trying to be stealthy here."

"Full voice again, Clebsy," Struggins said with a sigh.

"Oh, sorry, sir."

"Check the damn bathroom!"

She moved back into the main room and fixed her gaze down at the crack under the restroom door. There were shadows.

"The lifeforms are back, sir," Ewups announced urgently.

"Get out of there, soldier," Struggins commanded. "Mobilize! Mobilize!"

BACK HOME

"hat was simply the most amazing experience I've ever had," DeKella said as she and Harr materialized back in her bathroom.

"I'll bet that's not something you've ever thought you'd say while in the bathroom with a man."

She laughed in a snorting sort of way that Harr couldn't help but find endearing.

"I don't suppose I could go with you when you leave?" she asked suddenly. "It would sure make life more bearable than staying here and being known as a failure."

"Honestly," Harr replied, "I think you'd feel differently were you to spend even one day in our shoes."

"That bad?"

"Always seems to be." He went to open the door but stopped. "Remember that they're listening to everything we say when we're not in here."

"Got it."

They walked back out into the main room and looked around. There were fresh boot-prints on the carpet, the front door was slightly opened, and the smell of tortilla chips filled the air. That last note made very little sense to Harr. Whoever was in charge of training the strike team for this planet was clearly lacking in capability.

"Well," DeKella said, "that was quite something, Dr. Welder. You are an amazing lover."

Harr smiled, knowing that she was playing on the fact that the Kallian military was listening in. "I do what I can."

"You do quite well, indeed," she said as she walked over to the door. "Now, would you look at this? We seemingly left the door open in our rush of passion. I should close it quickly. We wouldn't want anyone *spying* on us, now would we?"

"That would be bad, yes."

"Speaking of spying, have you met General Struggins yet, Zep?"

"I don't believe I have, Rella."

"He's a fat old man who smells of mothballs," she said with a wicked grin. "Always in a sour mood, which I suppose should be expected after what I'd heard about him."

"Oh? What's that?"

"Someone had apparently spied on him for a couple of years before he made it to the rank of 13-Star General. I guess the military has a strong interest in knowing what's going on at all times, you know?"

"Interesting," Harr said. "What did they find?"

"It was a little disturbing, actually."

"Do tell."

"Well, the report was that they have footage of Struggins dancing naked at a campsite in the middle of winter while singing show tunes."

SPY SHOCK

hat's not true," Struggins yelped as Deddles and Ewups stared at him with wide eyes. They both seemed to be holding in their mirth. "I'm telling you it's a lie. I've never done such a thing! I don't even like camping."

"Whatever you say, sir," Deddles said, giggling.

"You've got to believe me," Struggins said, seeing his authority waning. "I wouldn't dance naked outside in the middle of winter. What sense would that make? And I haven't been camping since I was forced to do it during the terrorist crackdown back in 1411." He hoped that pointing out how he'd fought in an actual war would bring his underlings back into order. It didn't. "Now, I'll admit that I sing show tunes from time-to-time. But, really, who doesn't?"

Both of the young men raised their hands.

"Well, for my age group it's a very normal thing, but I would *never* do that in the nude."

"Not even in the shower, sir?" Deddles asked with a gleam in his eye.

"Okay, fair enough. In the shower I've sung a song or two. I'll admit that."

"Do you want me to continue recording all of this, sir?" Ewups asked while pointing at the little red blinking light on his screen.

"Recording it? You've been recording this entire surveillance?"

"Of course, sir. It's procedure."

"Are you insane?" Struggins bellowed. "Erase all of it, immediately. Pay special attention to that last bit, which, again, I attest was a patent fabrication."

STARTING THE TEST

The next morning put Harr and his crew in the lab of the W.A.R.P.E.D. building.

It was a madhouse of scientists, military personnel, reporters, and camera crews. Harr, Ridly, Jezden, and Vool tried to keep out of the way, but Harr knew he'd have to get into that room with the *Stewnathium Particles* before Rella could fire off the test. The problem was, how?

There were two scientists standing at the terminal next to the stairs that led up to the room. They obviously wouldn't be a problem. The two guards standing at the base of the stairs, however, probably would be.

Harr started looking around for another way into that room when General Struggins stepped right in front of him at the bequest of one of the reporters.

"I'm here with 13-Star General Laffable Struggins," the reporter said toward the camera in her pedantic way before turning to the general. "Sir, you have been a part of this project for a few years now. How do you feel things have progressed over that time?"

"More slowly than I would have liked, but that's usually the way of things."

"Do you anticipate any problems?"

"None. I have complete faith in Dr. DeKella and her crew of outstanding scientists. They've been working long hours to make sure everything is ready to go as planned. On top of that, I've brought in additional military police to watch all facets of this building until the test is done." He looked fixedly at Harr and added, "We wouldn't want anyone to do anything we might deem nefarious, after all."

The reporter turned back to the camera. "You heard it here, folks," she said. "General Struggins has placed security as a top priority."

"You can never be too safe with Kallian lives," Struggins noted proudly.

"Brilliantly stated," the reporter agreed. "On that point, I guess we can assume that the inspection phase went smoothly and that they've found nothing to cause too much concern?"

"Well," the general said with a grin as he motioned toward Harr, "why don't we just ask Dr. Welder over here directly?" Struggins walked over and offered his hand, which Harr reluctantly took. "I know we haven't been formally introduced," Struggins said, "but I would imagine that everyone knows about the famous Dr. Zep Welder."

"Never heard of him," the reporter said.

"I suppose I mean the people in the scientific community," Struggins amended.

"Ah, right." The reporter turned her attention to Harr. "Dr. Welder, you were responsible for the inspection of the systems here?"

"Uh…yes, right."

"And you expect everything to function as designed?"

He glanced at Struggins, who appeared to be hanging on

Harr's every word. "I can't say that for certain, but all of the failsafes and procedures check out."

"I'm curious, Dr. Welder," Struggins said, "how long have you been an inspector? I would imagine a very long time. I can't see them sending a rookie along for something so important, after all."

"Yes, it's been many years," Harr said worriedly.

"Maybe you could share with the world of Kallian some of the more prominent projects you worked on?"

"I wouldn't want to bore everyone," Harr said with a wave of his hand.

"I think it would be fascinating," the reporter said.

"Oh? Well, uh…let's see."

"Excuse me, everyone," DeKella announced, quieting the room and pulling the attention of the reporter and the cameraman away from Harr. "We are about to start the test."

Struggins moved to stand next to Harr. Out of the corner of his mouth, he said, "I know you're a fraud, Welder, or whatever your real name is. The real Welder and his crew never arrived. We don't know what you did with the actual inspectors, but you can be certain we'll find them. I also know all about your little attempt to sabotage this test."

"I don't know what you're talking about, General."

"Is that right? So you don't know about the charges that were placed in the lab?" Harr shook his head. "Come now, you're obviously the brains of this group."

"No idea what you're referring to."

"Well, no matter, we thwarted your little countdown already anyway. You could have at least used something complicated, but I guess going with the standard red-wire snip was all your meager team could muster. Fortunately, we caught it in time and connected those wires back up after your people left last night."

Harr turned to look at him. "You reconnected the wires?"

"Ahah," Struggins said with a winning grin, "looks like you *did* know about the charges." Harr bit his lip. "Of course I reconnected the wires. Everyone knows that if you clip the red wire it starts a countdown. Do you think I'm a first-year cadet, mister? And don't even think to try to clip them again. You won't have the chance. When this is all said and done, you'll get your comeuppance."

"Why wait?" Harr said, knowing that he could have Geezer teleport them off the planet anyway. Then he peered around at the cameras and the slew of reporters. "Ah, I see. You can't. If you do, you'll have egg on your face."

"What the hell is that supposed to mean?" Struggins said with a look of disgust. "Egg on my face? Who's ever heard of such a stupid thing?"

"It's just a saying where I come from. Means that you'll look foolish."

"You're talking about putting eggs on your face and you're calling *me* foolish?" Struggins signaled toward a few of his soldiers. "Take our 'inspectors' to that room up at the top of the stairs. They won't be able to do any harm from there. As soon as you have them secured, stand guard at the bottom of those stairs. If any one of them steps out, shoot them."

"Yes, sir."

Harr grinned as they were shuffled up to the very room that housed the *Stewnathium Particles*. He had been worried over how he was going to get into that room without drawing attention, but the general had unwittingly helped them do just that. As they moved into the room, Vool walked to the far wall and leaned against it. Unfortunately, since the wires had been refastened, her explosives were back in play.

"So, they're on to us," Ridly whispered, "but they put us in the room that we needed to be in to stop the test?"

"Struggins doesn't know how anything actually works," Harr replied, keeping his voice low. "He just thinks it's a safe place to house us while the test goes on. We have a bigger problem than stopping these particles, though."

"What?"

"Struggins got all of the wires reconnected on Vool's charges."

"What?"

"Apparently on this world," Harr explained, "cutting the red wires sets off a countdown for bombs."

"That's stupid."

"Agreed, but I'm sure a lot of things that we take for normal on Segnal would be stupid to these people."

"Well, what the hell are we going to do?" Ridly asked. "If Vool enters the destruct code on that little box of hers, we're done for."

Harr tapped his wristband. "Geezer?"

"Here, cap'n."

"Can you impair Vool's vision with those contact lenses that you gave her?"

"What do you mean?"

"You have to do something to mess up her vision."

"Yeah, I got that. What I'm asking is why?"

"The bombs are active again."

"Shit," Geezer said. "That's going to be...wait, I got it. It's like a camera lens, so I'll just zoom in and out over and over. That'll mess her up, big time. To make it even worse, I'll do each eye separately."

"Perfect."

Moments later, Vool grabbed the wall and started wavering. She was clearly about ready to wretch when she closed her eyes and steadied herself.

"What the hell is going on?" she said.

"It's working, Geezer," Harr said into his wristband.

"Captain Harr," Vool said icily, "are you trying to interfere with my mission?"

"I'm merely stopping you from interfering with mine, Vool."

"And you think you can outdo an Overseer with a simple set of contact lenses?" She laughed and reached under her eyelids and pulled the lenses out. "Idiot."

"Geezer," Harr said, defeated, "she pulled them out."

"Saw that, big cat."

"You and that bucket of bolts you call an engineer can't outwit me, Harr," Vool said snidely. "Your brains are the size of an atom compared to mine."

"Actually," Ridly interjected, "that makes zero sense. The size of your cranium is roughly the same as Captain Harr's, so, technically, your brain couldn't be much larger than his. If anything, I would wager it would be smaller, based on the visual comparison of your two skulls."

"I meant that my intellectual capacity is far superior to any stupid human's."

"You're a human also," noted Ridly.

"Humanoid," Vool corrected her, "not human."

"Ah."

"That broad is a real piece of shit," Geezer said into Harr's earpiece.

"Agreed, Geezer. She *is* a real piece of...uh...work."

Vool pushed off the wall and walked toward the window that overlooked the lab below. "Once I'm done blowing up this silly planet, I'm going to go up to that ship of yours, deactivate that stupid hunk of metal in your engineering department, and then I'll take your precious *Reluctant* back to the Overseers and we'll have a big parade where we'll melt it down in the volcano of my choosing."

How people like this ended up policing the universe seemed very...well, expected, actually. Harr didn't like it. Not that the Overseers would give a crap about what he thought, but he didn't like it.

"You never intended for us to succeed, did you?" Harr asked.

"Of course not. We wanted you to fail. We were just using you to show our people that we 'tried.'" She laughed. "Bunch of silly liberals."

"If you press that button," Ridly said, pointing at the box that Vool was holding, "aren't you going to blow up, too?

"I'm not as weak as you are, human," Vool said with a scoff. "I'll be off this rock and back on the *Reluctant* before the blast even reaches me. You see, we *have* transporter technology where I come from. Sadly, you won't live long enough to reach that level of advancement."

"Keep her talking, honcho," Geezer said in Harr's ear. "I've been working on a tweak to the transporter to get rid of the slowness. If it's as slow as it was with you when you were in that chick's bathroom, Vool will get out of it. Trying to make it instant."

"Sure it'll work?" Harr said, turning away so Vool couldn't hear him.

"It'll transport her for sure, but I don't know if the upgrades will get her to where she's going in one piece or not."

"Let's hope not." He spun back toward Vool and thought to incite her. "So, what makes you think you've the right to determine the destiny of other civilizations?"

"We're smarter than everyone?"

"Only because you stop everyone else from having a chance to usurp your power," he countered.

"Duh," she said with an 'are-you-stupid?' look on her face.

"My point, Vool, is that you're probably not as smart as you think you are. You're just smart enough to make it so nobody else ever gets to a point where they can eclipse your intellect."

"Again," she said, raising her eyebrows, "duh. I know what

you're trying to do, Harr, and it's not going to work. You're simply too dumb to outfox me, as you've adequately proved in your last two statements."

"One day you're going to meet your match, Vool."

She held her hands out in front of her and shook them around. "Am I shaking? I feel like I should be shaking." Then she dropped her hands and rolled her eyes at him.

"Smartass," Harr said.

"Better than being a dumbass," she noted.

"Almost there, prime," Geezer said. "Thirty seconds, tops."

Harr thought quickly. "You don't think we could take you out, Vool? There are three of us here."

"Oh, please," she said with a laugh. "I'd snap all three of your necks faster than you could even move. Especially you, Harr. You're slow as shit compared to these two."

"We're going to win, Vool, no matter what you do."

She shook her head. "Yeah, right. I'm sure that you'll just catch me off guard somehow. Like I'm stupid enough to fall for some trick by some inferior concoction of sub-par DNA." Suddenly, the detonator disappeared from Vool's hand. "What the hell?" she said and gawked at Harr with a face that spelled fear.

"Duh," said Harr with a smile an instant before her body faded out of view.

"Where did she go?" asked Jezden.

"Forgot to tell you that Geezer's transporter is working." Harr activated the speaker on his wristband. "She's gone, Geezer."

"Right on."

"Way to go, Geezer," Ridly said with a laugh.

"Thanks, queen bee," Geezer replied. "It was nothing."

"Where did you send her?" Harr asked.

"She's in the Multicombo Chamber."

"Ew," said Jezden.

"Didn't Dr. DeKella tell you that everything in there was going to melt down?" said Ridly.

"Instantly," Harr responded, feeling a twang of unexpected pleasure at knowing that Vool was no more. "I'm assuming the detonator is in there with her?"

"No, cap'n. I didn't want to chance her being able to activate it, so I sent it somewhere else."

"Where?"

"Honestly, I'm not sure. I just know it's not with her, prime."

"How are you not sure?"

"Because it was more important that she end up in that pot. I'm sure it's around there somewhere, but nobody knows how to use it but Vool, so I'm not worried.

"That's a pretty nasty way to go," Jezden said as he looked down toward the lab floor, "even if she did call me 'tiny tail' all the time."

"Get over it, already," Ridly said in a huff. "Your tail's not even real. Just let it go."

"Easy for you to say, Ridly. I'm used to getting laid all the time, but it's been damn near two days since my last session. Do you know what that can do to a mind like mine? Tack on top of that fact that everyone on this infernal planet thinks I have zero sexual prowess, and that gives me just enough ammunition to want to join Vool in that vat. I'm so damned horny right now that even Harr, here, looks appealing."

"Stand back, Jezden."

"I wasn't being serious," Jezden said with a grunt.

"Wait a minute," Harr said suddenly. "Did you just say that you haven't had relations in two days?"

"Yeah."

"That implies that you're having relations with someone on the ship. There are only two women on the *Reluctant*,

Ensign, and I'm certain that Lieutenant Moon isn't your type, which means…"

"It's obviously me, Captain," Ridly said nonchalantly.

"But you can't stand him!"

"True," she agreed with a shrug, "but the man's got talent."

"Okay, okay," Harr said, holding up his hands. "I'm sorry I asked. Still, I don't understand why there's a problem. You've both been together the entire time. If you've been getting it on with each other on the ship, why not get it on here, too?"

Ridly shook her head in surprise. "Dr. Baloo can't have sex with a *tiny tail*, Captain. That would be out of character!"

KEEPING AN EYE

Struggins couldn't help but wonder how Ewups thought he was doing what was demanded of him. All he had to do was keep an eye on the supposed inspectors, but the boy was standing at the window looking across at the room that housed the imposters. This would have made sense had that room not had the same one-way glass that the command room had.

"I thought I told you to keep an eye on those people, Ewups?" he said.

"Trying, sir."

"Why are you standing by the window, then?"

"So I can see them, sir."

"And, how, pray tell, are you able to see them, Ewups?" Struggins said, his voice beginning to rise. "Do you have some sort of special vision that allows you to see through the wrong side of one-way glass?"

"Uh…no, sir."

"Yet there you are, looking like a befuddled animal that's staring into the lights of an oncoming truck." Ewups glanced at the general with the look of an animal staring into the lights of an oncoming truck. Struggins sighed and shook his head. "Honestly, I have no idea why I bother. I also have no idea who the hell thought it would be a wise idea to put one-ways on that damn room in the first place. It's not a command room."

"It was a bundle deal, sir," Private Deddles offered. "The price to do two rooms was cheaper than one."

"Unbelievable, not to mention nonsensical. It would cost the manufacturer more...never mind. Mr. Ewups, my point in all of this is that you should just be sitting at your desk watching the video feed from that room."

"There are no cameras in that room, sir," Ewups replied like a man who knew what was coming.

"You're telling me that my lead technician," Struggins began, "the soldier who I put in charge of the surveillance for the most important project in the history of Kallian, decided that it was not in the best interest of this military to keep eyes on a room that has no other means of viewing?"

"That's correct, sir."

"Why the hell not?"

"I have no answer for that, sir."

"Well, then, Ewups, let me answer it for you. You didn't put cameras in there because you're a complete imbecile. Think that about nails it on the head?"

"Sorry, sir."

"I have a feeling that there might be a bit more delay on those papers sitting on my desk, Ewups."

Ewups' shoulders slumped as he sulked back to his desk.

In the event that this warp test was successful, Struggins was going to insist on building up a space fleet full of mentally fit, intelligent, qualified soldiers. No more getting in because your mother or father was a member of Parliament crap. Kallian's emissary fleet—meaning the fleet that was going to explore strange new worlds, seek out new civilizations, and blow the shit out of them—was going to be stocked with the best of the best. People like Struggins himself would have to be the baseline, though he had to admit that that was a tall order.

"Deddles," he said with hope, "please tell me that you cleared that room like I asked you to?"

"I did, sir," Deddles replied. "The only thing I found was this 12-inch pole."

"Finally, something was done correctly," Struggins said, feeling a bit of relief. "I don't know what the hell it's for," he said, looking it over, "but better to be safe than sorry."

THE TEST

*H*arr was looking out the window as Dr. DeKella continued her speech. She sounded tinny through the little speakers that were in the *Stewnathium Particles* room, and there was the slightest crackling sound. She kept looking up at the glass, and was clearly stalling for time.

"And now we approach the time for history to be made," she said insistently. "At the press of this button, the countdown to release the *Stewnathium Particles* will begin. Once released, they will mix in the Multicombo Chamber and a set of controlled explosions will occur. From that will come a magnetic field that shall expand and be focused around the metal box in Room C." She pointed. Heads and cameras jockeyed for position to catch a glimpse of the box. "If all goes as planned, the box will lift and move into a warp field."

"I don't see the damn pole, Captain," Ridly said frantically.

"She said it would be behind one of the pillars," Harr replied.

"I've checked them all."

"I re-checked them," Jezden added. "It ain't there."

Harr glanced up at the command room where Struggins was likely smiling smugly down upon him.

"Damn," Harr said. "Struggins must have gotten a hold of it."

"Well," DeKella said exasperatedly, "without further ado, I guess I'll go ahead and start the sequence."

Harr cringed as she reached out and pressed the button.

The sound of a computer voice filled the lab.

Chamber centrifuge activated. One hundred and eighty seconds until the Stewnathium Particles *are released. Please verify final procedural connections and secure Room C.*

"We have to block that damn feed," Harr said, pushing away from the window. "If we don't, we're all dead." Ridly and Jezden just stared at him. "Ideas?"

"We could transport back to the ship and hide from the Overseers," Ridly suggested.

"Doubt we'd be able to hide for long. You were there when they snapped us up in the first place, and Geezer hasn't been able to find that damn device that Frexle installed." He turned toward the ensign. "Jezden, do you have any ideas?"

"Hell, I don't know," he answered in frustration. "My head is a complete mess. Damn my programming!"

"Geezer?"

"I've been trying to get a lock on the *Stewnathium Particles* to see if I can just beam them out of that chamber, prime, but my transporter doesn't even recognize them and there's not enough time to alter that *Ridgway Converter* to guilt the tech into it."

"I'm on the call as well, sir," Sandoo announced. "I've been working with Moon, Curr, and Middleton, and the only thing we can think of is taking a targeted shot to knock out that building. It's not ideal, but it would guarantee a failure. We'd just have to transport you three back to the ship first."

"Except that those chemicals in those charges would likely mix during that explosion," Geezer pointed out. "That means a very large boom instead."

"Yes," Harr replied, "but you can beam those out."

"Good point, honcho. Hadn't thought of that."

"Actually, you should do that anyway, just in case."

"Consider it done. I'll put them somewhere deep in space."

Ninety seconds to Stewnathium Particle *release.*

Harr gazed out at Dr. DeKella. He hated the thought of it, but he felt that Sandoo and the rest of the team were correct. It was the only way out. There was ample justification for their position, too. Billions of lives were at stake. Losing thousands was awful, but to protect the masses, he would sacrifice the few. It was the only logical way.

Sixty seconds to Stewnathium Particle *release.*

"Come on, Ridly," Jezden was saying, which Harr was catching on the periphery of his thoughts, "what do you say? One last fling before time's up? You know it doesn't take me long to get this thing up and running, especially after two days of nothing."

Forty-five seconds to Stewnathium Particle *release.*

"That's it," Harr said as he spun and pointed at Jezden.
"What's it? Why are you pointing at me?"

GETTING TOGETHER

*H*arr sat on Dr. DeKella's couch as the two cuddled and watched the news. They had finally consummated their relationship. First they did it the Kallian way, which was oddly fun for Harr. Then he showed her how Segnalians got busy. She had enthusiastically approved.

"To call the warp test a failure," said Newscaster Melia Mekub, "would be a drastic understatement. The chamber that housed all of the necessary components completely melted down; the *Stewnathium Particles* turned out to be a complete flop; and the combination of items in that chamber somehow managed to produce strands of hair and bone fragments." Harr gagged at the knowledge of where those really came from. "Unfortunately, it's been reported that the components needed for that mix had taken years to cultivate, and that means that warp technology has been set back at least a full generation, assuming they can even gather together the funding to give it another shot. Contrary to what was first reported, though, it turns out that this was *not* the fault of any scientists on the project." Harr and DeKella both sat up at this statement. "It seems that the military commander in charge, a General Laffable Struggins, had sabotaged the entire thing."

The camera changed from the reporter to the scene of Struggins being dragged away by military police.

"I'm innocent, you fools!" he yelled as they pulled him toward an authority vehicle. "It was all a setup. Those weren't even the real inspectors. They did it! *They did it!*"

Melia Mekub returned to the screen. "General Struggins was also found to be carrying what appears to be a remote detonator in his coat pocket, though no bombs have been located as of yet."

Harr laughed out loud at that. Geezer was going to love the coincidence there.

"He'd placed bombs?" DeKella said, her mouth agape.

"No," Harr corrected, "Vool did."

"Oh."

"We knew she'd be up to no good, so we monitored her every move. As soon as she placed them, I had Ridly and Jezden…"

"Who?"

"Sorry, you know them as Drs. Baloo and Impotent."

"Ah, right."

"Well, they went in after and disarmed the explosives. Easy three-wire combination. You know, red, yellow, and green."

"Yes," she said with a nod, "it's on all the shows here. So you cut the yellow one?"

"No," Harr said, frowning. "We cut the red one. The yellow one just starts a thirty-minute timer."

"Really?"

"I thought everyone knew that, but after Struggins said that he'd pieced back the red wires that we'd cut, I had a feeling that something was amiss."

"Apparently we have different television shows."

A field reporter was on the screen next. He was asking questions to a young soldier who kept looking at the camera and smiling. Behind them was another, heavy-set soldier who was waving and saying, "Hi, Mom!" a lot.

"I'm here with Private Elderbung Deddles, the personal aide to General Struggins. Private Deddles, what can you tell us of the General's personality?"

"Well, sir," Deddles answered, "I've always thought that General Struggins was a bit strange, but I never would have imagined he'd do something like this. Of course, he was fond of saying that soldiers had to do what soldiers had to do in order for the military to advance, even if that meant bending the rules."

"You said that you felt he was strange, Private. How so?"

"I probably shouldn't say, but rumor has it that he likes to go camping in the middle of the winter, get naked, and dance around while singing show tunes."

Rella turned down the television and they both just sat there for a few minutes in awe.

"I have no idea how you managed to frame Struggins for all of this," she said in amazement, "but you've basically saved my career...not to mention my planet."

Harr grinned as the image of a proud robot filled his mind. "Just lucky, I guess."

"What I don't understand is how you blocked the *Stewnathium Particles* without that *Claythom Pole*?"

"As to that," Harr said with a laugh, "do you recall our short-tailed Dr. Impotent?"

DON'T WANT TO TALK ABOUT IT

I don't want to talk about it," Jezden said with his arms crossed.

"You should have seen him," Ridly continued without regard to his wishes. "It was quite impressive, truth be told. Actually, I'd even go as far as to say it was somewhat of a turn-on."

"Seriously?" Jezden said with a look of sudden interest.

"No, not seriously." She laughed, recalling the image of him blocking the *Stewnathium Particles* with his monstrous manhood. "You looked ridiculous!"

"Ugh. Can we just let this go, please? I mean, what I did saved billions of lives, right?"

"Yes, but I think we can all agree that with your lack of relations over the past two days, you would have stuck that thing in any opening that presented itself."

GOODBYES

*H*arr and DeKella had one final fling before he put his uniform back on and readied himself to return to duty.

"I hate to leave," he said, "but I really need to get back to my ship."

"Will I see you again?"

"I'll make it a point to stop by Kallian as often as possible."

"Talk about a long-distance relationship," she said with a sad smile.

"True."

"It's a shame. For someone who has no clue about our sexual function, you were the best lover I've ever had."

"Honestly," Harr said with a shrug, "I think it's just that you guys are too limited in what you find appealing. All I did was bring the ruckus to you in the same way that Segnalians do it. We like things such as breasts and legs. Frankly, I'm not even considered very good at this sort of thing on my planet."

She gaped at him. "You've just made a great point. I could show your techniques to the world. It'll be a sexual revolution. I'll make millions!"

Harr was both happy and sad about this revelation. On the one hand, he would be considered the man who brought a new level of sexual satisfaction to the world of Kallian; on the other hand, he would soon be relegated to being a below-average lover on yet another planet.

"But what about your science?" he asked.

She folded her hands together and looked down at them before releasing what appeared to be a defeated sigh.

"I guess now's as good a time as any to confess something to you," she said solemnly.

"Uh oh."

"Let me put it this way: You guys showed up at precisely the right time."

"We did?"

"Yeah." She laughed in a not-so-funny way. "Truth is that I have no idea what would have happened had those *Stewnathium Particles* made it through."

"What?"

"I had my guesses, sure, and my mathematical model was pretty solid, but I can't help but think that it would have failed horribly anyway." She shrugged. "That's one mystery I'm glad will never be solved. At least not in my lifetime."

"Amazing."

VELI IS LIKABLE

"They killed her, Frexle," Veli said with a sense of distress, "and she'd never even gotten me the details on their technology. Stupid bitch."

"Yes, Lord Overseer, which only serves to prove that they are worthy to work for us, and Vool was clearly not."

Veli tapped on his desk a few times. "I have to admit that you have a valid argument there."

"Thank you, my lord."

"And you say that our people are happy with this lack-of-violence outcome?"

"Your support among the populace has improved by nearly fifteen percent. That is quite significant, my lord."

"So you're saying that...well...they *like* me?"

"Fifteen percent more of them do than they did yesterday, my lord," Frexle affirmed. "Now, I'm sure that the numbers may have received a one- to two-percent bump due to the posters that Senators Pookand, Calloom, and Kleeve put together." Then, recalling the news report he'd seen moments before entering the Lord Overseer's office, he added, "May they rest in peace."

"Fifteen percent, eh?" Veli said, clearly not caring about the assassinations of three of his cabinet members. "That's something, at least."

"I'd argue that it's excellent, sir."

"This being the case," said Veli in a tone of declaration, "I command that we keep this Platoon F crew of yours around for a little while longer. Maybe they can help bump my popularity up even more in the coming year."

"Excellent, my lord."

"I'll just need to find some other means of sating my bloodlust, and the bloodlust of all of our *DeathToAllCompetitors* political party."

"I'm certain you'll find a way, my lord. You are rather clever, after all."

"And likable," Veli stated. "Let's not forget likable."

"Yes, that too."

DEBRIEFING

he *Reluctant* arrived at the Overseers' base without a fuss. Harr had instructed the crew to keep the transporter device under wraps for now. He didn't want the Overseers finding any new concerns toward keeping Platoon F around. Geezer had said that he'd contacted Goozer to share how he'd managed to get the device working. Harr thought it was great that the two engineers stayed in contact. It had proved beneficial more than once.

Frexle was on board, again sitting in Harr's chair. The man seemed rather pleased indeed. Harr assumed that the death of Vool was a big contributor to his mood.

"You are just as resourceful a crew as I had imagined," Frexle stated. "More so, if I were being truthful."

"Thank you, sir," Sandoo said with a salute.

"What's with the hand-on-the-head thing?"

"Just a salute, sir. A means of respect."

"I like that, Commander," Frexle said with a satisfied smile. "Keep doing it."

"Yes, sir," Sandoo said, saluting again. Harr knew that the commander loved protocol.

"They are a top-notch bunch," Harr said. "That's for sure."

"Especially your man who had the willingness to put his junk in the way of progress. I daresay you saved an entire world with your pecker, young man."

"Yeah, right," Jezden said with a grunt.

"And you all managed to kill Vool, too." Frexle clapped heartily. "Hell, that alone would have made this crew heroes in my book. Who knew that you humans could be so powerful? You seem very fleshy and pointless—no offense."

"We're not all human," Geezer stated through the speaker.

"Ah, yes, my apologies. How could I forget your robotic mastermind? If only there were more like him."

"We're not human either," said Ridly.

"Pardon?"

"We're androidth," Moon added.

"Androidth?"

"Androids, sir," Sandoo clarified.

Frexle jumped out of his chair and walked up to Harr, looking him over in a studious way.

"Amazing," he said after a time. "I mean, I should have known. That superhero look alone…"

"I'm human," Harr said with a grimace.

"But…"

"The rest of us are androids, sir," Sandoo said.

"So that's why you were all able to perform so well during boot camp," Frexle said while appraising Sandoo. "It also explains why Harr, here, didn't do as well. He couldn't keep up. Makes one wonder why he's in charge."

"Because he's the only one who can think outside of the box, sir," Sandoo answered. "We aren't quite as capable of doing that, but we are told that we are learning, sir."

"Interesting," Frexle said as he studied them all again. "Androids. Amazing. You know, I think that we should keep that bit of information between us. It may prove dangerous should any of the other Overseers learn of this."

Harr moved to his chair and sat down before Frexle could regain the spot. "So now what?" he asked.

"Simple," Frexle said. "We wait for the next event to unfold. They happen pretty frequently. There's always someone out there getting caught in the process of advancement."

"Until then, how about letting my team get a little R and R?"

"Rest and relaxation, right?"

"Correct."

"I've been trying to get your vernacular down," Frexle said conspiratorially. "I've even been watching some of those *Stellar Hike* episodes that your engineer suggested. Amazing stuff."

"Told ya, big cat," said Geezer through the speaker.

"You did, indeed. It turned me on to a bunch of other shows too. One of my favorites being *Dr. Huh*. Clever writing in that, even if the sets are lacking."

"Yeah, and those *Phallics* are amazing."

"Agreed," Frexle said and then gave one last look around. "Again, you all did a fantastic job." He snapped his fingers. "By the way, what did you do with the explosives that Vool had placed?"

"Took care of it, boss," Geezer said. "I trans..."

"Uh," Harr interrupted loudly before Geezer could let the cat out of the bag regarding their transporter technology, "we made a stop-off somewhere deep in space on the way back and jettisoned them."

"Yeah, right," Geezer said quickly. "What the cap'n said."

"I see." Frexle held eye contact with Harr for moment. "You're sure about this?"

"Positive, sir," Harr stated, returning the stare.

"Somewhere deep in space?" Frexle asked skeptically.

"Right," Harr answered after swallowing. "Somewhere deep in space."

Frexle finally broke the connection and shrugged. "As you say, then." Harr slowly released his breath. It was obvious that Frexle was one of those bosses who knew when to press a point and when to let it go. "Oh, before I forget, Drill Sergeant Razzin wanted me to tell you that he still thinks you're a waste of space and that he's ready for a rematch any time you're interested."

Harr shook his head and laughed.

"Oh, and Corporal Woor said that, per regulation 5221M, if I recall correctly, you are not a waste of space, but rather a very important and respected individual."

"Incredible," Harr replied.

Frexle smiled and rubbed his hands together. "Until next time, then, I shall bid you adieu."

He vanished, leaving the crew standing around in silence.

"Turned out not to be such a bad guy," Geezer said. "At first I thought he was kind of a dumbass."

"As you put it earlier, Geezer," Harr said, "I've had worse bosses."

"Yep."

Harr rapped his fist on the Captain's chair and breathed in the familiar ship air. "I don't know about the rest of you, but I'd like to surprise a particular doctor on Kallian and have a solid week of non-stop relations with her."

"Sounds good," said Jezden. "Count me in."

"Hah hah," Harr replied dryly. "She's not interested in small-tails, Ensign."

"Low blow, Captain."

"I think I'd like to hit *Fantasy Planet*, personally," Ridly said.

"Me, too," Moon agreed.

"I'm in," Ensigns Curr and Middleton said simultaneously.

"Sounds good," Jezden said resignedly. "Maybe I'll set up something where Kallians like small tails."

"Man," Ridly said, "you've really got issues."

"What about you, Commander?" Harr asked.

Sandoo seemed a bit uncomfortable at the suggestion. "I'll probably just stay with the ship or something."

"Everyone needs a little time away, Commander," Harr said. "You should go to *Fantasy Planet* with the rest of the crew. You can request anything, you know. Heck, you could even lead a battalion or fight in a war, or whatever you want."

"Really?"

"That's kind of the point of the planet, Sandoo."

"Then heck yeah, I'm in! ... uh, sir."

"Excellent. Geezer?"

"You know me, chief," Geezer answered. "I'm tethered to the *Reluctant*. Besides, I'm happiest here. Bad shit always happens when I'm not on board. Fact is that when you're all gone, that's kind of a vacation for me."

"All right, then," Harr said. "Whenever you're ready, Geezer, plot the coordinates for *Fantasy Planet*. We'll drop off the crew there first and then you can take me on to Kallian."

"Coordinates are plotted, prime."

Captain Harr beamed as he glanced around the bridge of his ship, pointed to the main screen and said, "Press it down."

Nothing happened.

"Sorry, honcho, but did you just say, 'Press it down?'"

"No good?" Harr said as he shifted in his seat. "Just trying to come up with my own captain-y way of telling you to launch. With all that talk about *Stellar Hike* over the last couple of days, it got me thinking that all the cool starship commanders have their own signature way of doing that.

Captain Quirk from *Stellar Hike* always said, 'Warp speed ahead!' Captain Prickhard from *Stellar Hike: The New Crew Aboard* just motioned his hand forward and said, 'Engage.' I'm just trying to find my personal way of doing it."

"Gotcha. Well, 'press it down' is okay, I guess. It's a little lacking, but it's not awful."

"How about 'slam it'?" suggested Jezden.

"Go forth!" Sandoo offered.

"Thmack it!" said Moon.

"Let's scoot on outta here," Curr said.

"Fire the engines!" Middleton chimed in.

"Move out!" Ridly added.

"Hmmm," Geezer said after a few moments. "I suppose you could just go simple and say, 'Hit it.' It's kind of what I do anyway. Well, actually, I duck under the table, reach up, and hit it, but that's kind of lengthy."

"Why do you duck under the table?"

"Because I still don't trust the damn thing," Geezer answered.

"That's disheartening," said Harr.

"Yep."

"Fine," Harr said after deciding that this time he was going to put his seatbelt on *before* it was necessary. Once it clicked into place, he said, "Everyone ready?"

They all nodded.

"Good." He stared up at the screen, recognizing that even though they had a new employer, they were still the same team, and he appreciated each and every one of them. Even Jezden, but only because he had just been responsible for using his tally-whacker to save an entire planet. "Okay, Geezer?"

"Yeah, big cat?"

"Hit it!"

SOMEWHERE DEEP IN SPACE

*U*ltra Commander Foom Aglian sat in his chair on the bridge of his ship, *The Foom's Vengeance*, overlooking the flurry of activity of his crew. They were running back and forth, filling out forms, checking systems, and generally preparing for the battle to come.

The main screen showed the planet of *Yalwoogar* at 5,000-times zoom. It appeared to be directly in front of the ship, but they were still four hours away. Ultra Commander Foom Aglian allowed himself a moment of bliss in knowing that soon another world would fall to his crushing army. He so loved destroying planets. His favorite part was when they sent in the invading forces and started tearing the native inhabitants to bits as they screamed in horror. It made him giggle so.

"Number one," he yelled in his booming voice.

"Yes, Ultra Commander Foom Aglian," said his second-in-command, a middle-aged man who stood tall and proud, with sufficient facial scarring that proved his worth in battle.

"Are all of the ships prepared for the connection protocol?"

"We are starting the connection now, sir."

"Put it on screen."

Yalwoogar was soon replaced by the beauty of the Foom Fleet. The entirety of their civilization had left the world of Foom, leaving it desolated and lifeless, deciding instead to live out their days in the vastness of space. No more were they tied down to any one planet. Instead, they hunted worlds with thriving civilizations, studied them, and then destroyed them with glee.

Basically, the Fooms were downright bastards, and that made Ultra Commander Foom Aglian proud indeed.

The Foom Fleet consisted of twenty warships that, when connected, looked somewhat like a small moon. In this formation, a vast shield was deployed that handled the duty of protecting the main ship. On top of that, it allowed weapons to be fired from any point, all facing outward, of course.

To the right of the main screen hung a detailed painting of Ultra Commander Foom Aglian. His scars were legendary, especially the one that ran from the top of his skull, down across his eye, and ending at the edge of his chin. That scar had been given to him by his father, former Ultra Commander Foom Equid, on the night of the ascension battle. All of Equid's sons had died in that battle, except for Aglian. He had used skill and cunning in his battle, just as he had done in every battle since. Muscle could only get you so far against muscle, but creativity gave an edge that ended Equid and set Aglian as the new Ultra Commander of Foom.

The sound of clanking metal reverberated throughout the ship as the connections continued.

"Sir," said Number One, "the connections are going as planned. Do you still wish to have the main relays connected for a full assault?"

"I've been thinking about that," he replied without

looking at his officer. "We know that these *Yalwoogarians* are a pacifist people, right?"

"Yes, sir."

"No weaponry at all, correct?"

"None that we could determine, sir."

"Wouldn't it be fun, then, to just land on the planet and take them in one-to-one fashion?"

His officer grinned. "Just like the old days, sir."

"Exactly. It's not very often that we get to beat-up on a defenseless world, after all."

"That's true, sir."

"Just like those public service commercials on the video channels always say, 'Bullying is right and good, everyone should do it.'"

"Wonderful commercials, sir."

"Except that not everyone can do it," noted Ultra Commander Foom Aglian. "If they could, there wouldn't be any bullies because they'd have nobody to push around."

"Hadn't thought of that, sir."

"That's why I'm the Ultra Commander, Number One," he said off-handedly as he noticed something different on his bridge. Sitting off in the corner were three small white boxes. They each had a little tube on their bottom sides and three wires connecting from one hemisphere to the other. "What are those boxes, Number One?"

His first officer walked over to the boxes and carried them back. He then summoned Science Officer Foom Chipklo for a look.

"What do you suppose these are?" Ultra Commander Foom Aglian asked.

"They look like bombs to me, sir," Chipklo replied, twisting one of the devices in his hand while studying it from all angles.

"Where do you suppose they came from?"

"I couldn't say, sir."

"My guess, sir," said Number One, "is that the *Yalwoogar* are more resourceful than we had originally assumed."

"You think they put these on my ship?"

"I can't imagine anyone else who would have, sir."

"But we are still four hours away from them, Number One."

"Yes, sir."

This gave Ultra Commander Foom Aglian pause. If these *Yalwoogar* had some means of transporting explosives to his ship from that distance, then maybe they were much worthier foes than he had expected.

"Search all ships immediately and tell me if any more of these things are found."

Two hours later, Number One reported back that no other bombs had been located. That made the point even more telling. These damned *Yalwoogarians* had not only sent the bombs along, they purposefully targeted *his* ship in the process. He smiled at this.

"We may have a worthy foe, yet, Number One."

"Yes, sir."

"The question now is why haven't they activated these things?"

"Couldn't say, sir."

"It could be that they need to be closer to active them, sir," offered Chipklo.

"You're saying that they could transport those bombs to us from four hours away, but they can't activate them from that far out?"

"It's just a thought, sir."

"And a stupid one at that." He signaled two of his security officers over. When they arrived, he said, "Take Science Officer Chipklo below and beat him with a whip rod until he passes out, and then throw him into space."

"But, sir, I was just…"

"Do you want me to make your sentence worse, Chipklo?"

"Worse than beating me unconscious and then throwing me into space, you mean?"

"Precisely."

"I'm not sure how you could make that worse. I mean…"

"Silence!" One of the guards punched Chipklo, knocking him to his knees.

"Well done, guard. Take him below and beat him unconscious, as I had previously commanded. But then wake him up, and stick his right foot out of the airlock for thirty seconds. Then chop it off. Do the same thing to his other foot. Repeat this with his hands. After that, throw his whole body out into space while he's still awake." He turned to look at Chipklo with challenging eyes. "Does that sound worse?"

"Yes, sir," Chipklo replied with a look of admiration. "Your wisdom knows no bounds, sir."

"Oh, it's nothing," Ultra Commander Foom Aglian replied with a wave of his hand. "I just have loads of practice, is all. Now, take him away."

As they dragged the science officer out of the room, Number One held up one of the bombs and said, "What should we do with these, sir? Chipklo was our best bomb tech."

"Oh, we don't need him. It's obvious what we have to do."

"It is?"

"Of course, Number One. You've seen plenty of television shows in your youth, yes?"

"Yes, sir," Number One replied. "My favorite was *Space Blood Expedition*."

"The original or *The Younger Crew*?"

"The original for me, sir."

"I preferred *The Younger Crew*, myself. Probably because

the special effects were better. Though I must admit that I enjoyed *The Problem with Pubbles* episode from the original series."

"That was a classic, sir."

"Anyway, let's get back to this bomb before it detonates." He reached out and snatched one away from his first officer.

"Do you know how to defuse it, sir?"

"Come now, Number One, you just said that you enjoyed watching *Space Blood Expedition*."

"Yes, sir?"

"Well, think back on that and use your senses, man."

Number One could only furrow his brow and blink a few times in response.

"It's easy," Ultra Commander Foom Aglian stated as he pulled forth his knife. "You've got a bomb here with three wires: red, yellow, and green. Everyone knows that you always cut the green one."

Thanks for Reading

If you enjoyed this book, would you please leave a review at the site you purchased it from? It doesn't have to be a book report... just a line or two would be fantastic and it would really help us out!

John P. Logsdon
www.JohnPLogsdon.com

John was raised in the MD/VA/DC area. Growing up, John had a steady interest in writing stories, playing music, and tinkering with computers. He spent over 20 years working in the video games industry where he acted as designer and producer on many online games. He's written science fiction, fantasy, humor, and even books on game development. While he enjoys writing lighthearted adventures and wacky comedies most, he can't seem to turn down writing darker fiction. John lives with his wife, son, and Chihuahua.

Christopher P. Young

Chris grew up in the Maryland suburbs. He spent the majority of his childhood reading and writing science fiction and learning the craft of storytelling. He worked as a designer and producer in the video games industry for a number of years as well as working in technology and admin services. He enjoys writing both serious and comedic science fiction and fantasy. Chris lives with his wife and an ever-growing population of critters.

CRIMSON MYTH PRESS

Crimson Myth Press offers more books by this author as well as books from a few other hand-picked authors. From science fiction & fantasy to adventure & mystery, we bring the best stories for adults and kids alike.

Check out our complete book catalog:

www.CrimsonMyth.com

Printed in Great Britain
by Amazon